KNIT ONE MURDER TWO

A Knitorious Murder Mystery

REAGAN DAVIS

M-1

COPYRIGHT

Sign up for Reagan Davis' email list to be notified of new releases: https://dl.bookfunnel.com/pqrgvh5976

ISBN: 978-1-9990435-3-7 (ebook)

ISBN: 978-1-9990435-2-0 (print)

CONTENTS

CHAPTER 1

I toss the last pillow onto the bed then stand back, squint, and scan the duvet cover for creases and bumps. One small bump catches my eye. I give the edge of the duvet a gentle tug and run my hand across the smooth surface, pleased with my neatly made bed. What feels more satisfying than climbing into a comfortable, well-made bed at the end of a long day? Not much.

In theory, making half a bed should take half the time it takes to make an entire bed, but that isn't how it works. At least not for me. I take the same amount of time to make half a bed as I do to make an entire bed. My bed-making skills are an example of Parkinson's Law: "Work expands to fill the time available for its completion." In other words, I expand the time it takes to make half of the bed into the time that it takes to make the entire bed.

See also: the junk in my junk drawer expands to fill the entire drawer, my yarn stash expands to fill all the available storage in my house, and my wardrobe expands to fill the entire closet when my husband and his wardrobe move out of the master bedroom and into the guest bedroom across the hall.

I pull my favourite jeans from my drawer and my plum-coloured top from my closet. I get dressed, return my housecoat to its hook in the washroom, then open the washroom window to let the fresh air clear the lingering steam from my shower. I apply tinted moisturizer with SPF 30 to my face, a bit of mascara around my hazel eyes, and smear on some lip balm. My chestnut-brown hair is still wet from the shower. It's too early to tell if today will be a good-curl day or a bad-curl day, so I slip a hair band on my wrist in case it's a bad-curl day. I unplug my phone and leave my bedroom with coffee on my mind.

Walking past Adam's room, his unmade bed catches my eye, and I close the door so I don't have to see it. "Just a few more weeks, Megan," I mutter to myself. "I just have to hang in there for a few more weeks." Now that Hannah has graduated from high school and we've dropped her off at university, he can focus on finding an apartment. With any luck, he'll be out of here by the first of the month.

Like a woman on a mission, I walk into the kitchen and straight to the coffee maker, pop a pod of caramel coffee in the machine and place my *I'd rather be knitting* mug under the spout.

While waiting for the coffee to brew, I walk over to the kitchen table and open my planner to today's date. I have a 10 a.m. fundraising committee meeting at the Animal Centre, and I work from 1 p.m. to 5 p.m. I've been working part-time at Knitorious, Harmony Lake's only knitting store and my second home, for just over five years.

I check the clock on the microwave and see it's 8:30 a.m. now, so I have an hour to enjoy my coffee and some knitting before I leave.

I collect the full mug from the machine and settle myself in my favourite corner of the family-room sofa, cross my legs, and tuck my feet under me like a little kid in kindergarten who's waiting for story time. I place my phone on the armrest.

"Oscar, play my playlist," I announce to the empty room.

"OK," Oscar replies.

A few seconds later, thanks to the miracle of modern technology, Gwen Stefani's voice fills the previously quiet space.

Oscar is a digital voice assistant. Hannah and Adam gave him to me for Mother's Day. They both love technology. Most holidays I can look forward to getting their new favourite gadget. They make me look more tech-savvy than I actually am.

Oscar is useful. He can play music, keep my grocery list, give weather updates, read news headlines, remind me when the laundry is finished, look up phone numbers, and other Internet-based tasks. He is the size of a hockey puck and sits stoically on the end table beside my sheep-shaped yarn bowl, waiting silently for someone to say his name and ask him to do something. He's like a useful pet that never needs to be fed or watered.

I take a moment to savour my much anticipated first

sip of coffee. I follow the warmth as it travels down my throat and spreads through the rest of my body. I put the mug back on the coaster and take my knitting from the yarn bowl.

Ding!

The vibration of my phone makes the sofa shake. It's a text message from a number I don't recognize. I pick up my phone and use my fingerprint to open the screen.

Mystery texter: Hi Mrs. Martel. My name is Fred Murphy. My wife, Stephanie, works with Adam and they've been having an affair.

I didn't see that coming. How did he get my number?

He sends a second message, a screenshot of a rather intimate text conversation, presumably between Adam and Stephanie. I know text conversations can be easily faked, but my instincts tell me there's something to this.

Our marriage has been over for months and Adam is home less than ever, even for a workaholic lawyer. Since Hannah left home a few weeks ago, some nights he comes home so late and leaves so early in the morning that I'm not certain he came home at all.

A third text:

Can we meet to discuss? I have more proof but I'd like to discuss it with you in person. I can come to Harmony Lake. Let me know when and where.

I immediately text my best friend, April:

Adam's having an affair!

I attach the screenshot of the steamy text exchange that Fred sent to me and hit send.

Me: Her husband wants to meet me. Says he has more

tell me.

April texts me back right away:

Wow! Do you want to meet him?

That's a good question. I'm not sure. My curiosity is piqued, that's for sure, and there must be a reason he's reaching out to me. I feel like I should meet him.

April: Somewhere public. Meet him at the bakery so T and I can keep an eye on him.

April and her wife, Tamara, own Artsy Tartsy, the bakery up the street from Knitorious. Tamara is a talented pastry chef, and I stop by to taste her creations every chance I get.

I reply to Fred:

Noon at Artsy Tartsy?

Fred: See you then.

I put my phone down on the armrest of the sofa and pick up my knitting. I'm working on a sock in plain stockinette stitch, a perfect project for knitting in front of the TV or trying to process your feelings about your soon-to-be-ex-husband possibly having a girlfriend. A married girlfriend.

I find my rhythm quickly, and I'm automatically working one stitch after another while thinking about the text conversation I just had with Fred Murphy.

Is there an appropriate reaction to finding out your soon-to-be-ex-husband might be seeing someone? I'm not angry. I don't feel betrayed. I'm shocked. It hadn't occurred to me that Adam might be seeing someone, much less someone who's married.

Ding! Dong!

After about twenty rounds of knitting and navel gazing, the sound of the doorbell brings me back to the here and now. It's April. I know before I put my knitting back in the yarn bowl and get to the door that it's her. I know because I would do the same thing in her shoes; I'd rush straight over to her to make sure she's OK.

April and I have been friends for sixteen years. We met at a mommy-and-me group when Adam, Hannah, and I first moved to Harmony Lake. April and Tamara's daughter, and my Hannah are the same age and best friends. The girls both just started university in Toronto. As difficult as it is to send your child off to school in the big city, April and I find comfort knowing both we and the girls have each other to make the transition easier.

I open the door. April comes in and I close it behind her. We have a tight hug, and when we pull away from each other, she hands me a small white confectionery box.

"It's a maple carrot cupcake with pecans, topped with maple cream cheese frosting. T is thinking of adding them to the fall menu and wants your opinion."

"Halfsies?" I ask her over my shoulder.

I'm already halfway to the kitchen to get a plate.

"No, thank you! I've had at least a dozen of them while she's been perfecting the recipe. I've eaten so many, I dreamed I was being chased by maple carrot cupcakes, and they were pelting me with pecans."

"All the more for me!" I sit down at the kitchen table and open the box. "She's outdone herself, April. It's almost too pretty to eat. Almost."

I carefully start to peel the paper liner away from the

cupcake, and April takes a seat at the table across from me.

"So," she asks, "how are you doing? Have you heard anything else from Fred?"

My mouth is full, so I shake my head while I chew.

When my mouth is empty, I say, "I knew it would happen eventually. It's not like I expect him to spend the rest of his life alone because our marriage didn't work out. I'm just shocked he didn't wait until he moved out, you know? And she's married."

April nods her head and looks at me intently.

April and I are physical opposites. I'm short with an hourglass figure. She's tall and lean. I'm a curly-haired brunette with hazel eyes, while she is a straight-haired blonde with blue eyes. I have fair skin, but she has a perpetual, year-round sun-kissed glow.

"We haven't even told anyone yet," I say. "Other than Hannah, the only people who know we're separated are you and Connie."

Connie is my boss at Knitorious, but she's more like family than a boss.

I finish my cupcake and ask April to please tell T to add it to the menu. It's fabulous and needs to be shared with the entire town as soon as possible. I put my plate in the dishwasher and get a glass of water, then I walk back to the table and sit down.

"I'm not in love with him anymore." This is the first time I've said it out loud, and as soon as I say it, it feels honest and I feel a little unburdened. "I love him because he's Hannah's dad, and the three of us will always be a family, you know? But our marriage is definitely over."

My lack of intense feelings about Fred's texts help to confirm this for me.

I'm mindlessly twirling my wedding ring with my right hand. I'm a fidgeter, and if I'm not knitting, my hands find something else to do to keep busy. April reaches across the table and takes my hands.

"OK, Megan, but can I ask you one question? If your marriage is over, and you're OK with that, why are you still wearing your wedding ring?" She picks up my left hand and shows it to me as if she's trying to prove I'm wearing it.

The ring is a thick band of white gold with a row of square and marquis-cut amethysts—my birthstone—in the centre and a row of diamonds above and below it.

"We're both still wearing our rings. We decided we'd wear them until we start to tell people. It was part of the plan not to ruin Hannah's senior year of high school." I shrug. "Also, I love this ring. I designed it myself. When we got married, we were so young and poor that we couldn't afford an engagement ring. We had simple white gold wedding bands. Adam always wanted to upgrade my ring, so for our 10th anniversary he told me to pick a ring, and I designed this one."

I slip the ring from my left hand to my right hand, and surprisingly, it fits perfectly, like it's meant to be worn there.

"Better?" I ask, holding my right hand in front of April's face.

"As long as you're happy." She smiles and stands up. "Are you ready to head to the bakery and meet Fred?"

CHAPTER 2

IT'S A BEAUTIFUL, sunny day, so we decide to walk to Artsy Tartsy. The breeze coming off the lake is just cool enough to be refreshing, and the warm sun on my face is a reminder that soon the weather will change. I'll miss walking to Water Street without having to bundle up in a coat, mitts, and winter boots.

Water Street is to Harmony Lake what Main Street is to other small towns. It's our main drag, our downtown, and where many of the town's businesses and stores are located. Most of the buildings on Water Street are on the north side of the street. The south side is a strip of park in front of the boardwalk and lake front.

Weather permitting, I prefer to walk to work because it's only about a ten-minute walk from my house. Harmony Lake is a small town, both geographically and in population, so almost anywhere you need to go is within walking distance. The town is nestled snugly between the lake on the south, and the Harmony Hills mountain range on the north. Nature left no room for expansion but provided the town with the perfect foundation for a tourism-based economy.

The Harmony Hills mountain range has two popular ski resorts that are usually fully booked all winter with skiers and snowboarders, and fully booked again in the summer with city-escapees who flock to the lake front.

Except for a few weeks in the fall and a few weeks in the summer, the town is full of tourists. During the busiest weeks, I think there are more visitors than locals in Harmony Lake.

Autumn is my favourite time of year here because the town is so pretty with the fall colours on the trees. The storefronts also have their fall window displays set up, and arrangements of pumpkins and fall flowers are dotted throughout the town. The weather isn't too hot or too cold, and since the summer tourist season is over and the winter tourist season hasn't begun, for a few precious weeks, we locals have the town to ourselves.

When we get to Water Street, we cross the street on the south side and go through the park. A few boats dot the lake near the horizon line, and the park is full of neighbours who are out and about enjoying the beautiful day. I can feel my phone vibrating in my pocket. It's Adam. I don't have the mental bandwidth to deal with him right now, so I clear the notification from my phone and return it to my pocket.

I glance to my right, across the street, and spot Paul Sinclair walking along the sidewalk in front of The Pharmer's Market, the local pharmacy.

"Shoot!" I say.

I duck back behind April, then leap to her left side where I'm hoping her height will shield me from Paul's view.

"What is it?" She asks, confused by my sudden ducking and weaving around her.

"It's Paul Sinclair," I reply. "I was supposed to attend a fundraising meeting at the Animal Centre this morning, and with all the kerfuffle, I totally forgot. I didn't even think to call and let them know I wouldn't make it. You know how he is."

I crane my neck backwards to sneak a peek across the street behind April's back, hoping Paul has moved along without spotting me. I'd rather deal with him after this meeting with Fred.

It's too late. Paul is crossing the street. He saw me, and now he's catching up with me, probably to scold me for my thoughtlessness and lack of respect for the other committee members who did attend the meeting. I can already hear it, and he's not even here yet.

In addition to being a member of the Town Council, Paul Sinclair is also the president of the Water Street Business Association (known by the locals as the WSBA), the town council representative on the WSBA board, the WSBA representative on the Town Council, and a member of every other committee, organization, and community group in town. To say he's involved in the town is an understatement.

He's also the town's self-appointed, unofficial bylaw officer. He has the remarkable ability to recite any town bylaw by heart and takes it upon himself to enforce them whenever he deems anyone to be violating one, no matter how small the violation or how justified the action. Basically, he's the town bully. He doesn't seem threatening at first, but if you violate a bylaw, miss a committee meeting, or otherwise displease him, he'll make sure you know it.

He's tall with perfect posture, a year-round tan, and unnaturally white teeth that are almost always on display with a carefully molded, wide smile that reminds me of the smile a fairy-tale wolf has before he eats you or blows your house down.

He even manages to maintain his smile when he's in bully-mode, which is confusing and insulting when you're his target. I've only ever seen him wear a suit, and his dark hair is always perfectly coiffed, probably because his wife, Kelly, is also his hairdresser, and the owner of Hairway To Heaven, our local hair salon.

"Megan!" He's almost caught up to us now. April and I stop and turn around.

My phone is vibrating. It's Adam again. I reject the call and drop the phone in my tote bag.

"Hi Paul." I sigh. "Listen, I'm sorry I missed the fundraising meeting at the Animal Centre this morning. There's been a..."

I've drawn a blank. What do you call an unexpected text message from your husband's potential girlfriend's husband?

"...family emergency...and it took over my day. The meeting completely slipped my mind."

You could call it a family emergency; that seems about right to me.

"Oh no! Is Hannah OK? Is anyone hurt or anything damaged?" He asks, somehow managing to sound compassionate and concerned even when he's making me feel like an irresponsible loser.

His smile stays constant. Not a wince.

"Yes," I reply, knowing full well this is a set-up. "Everyone is fine, no one is hurt and nothing is damaged. It isn't that type of emergency."

I attempt my own toothy grin and tilt my head as I look up at him.

"Well, that's a relief! If someone was hurt, I could understand you failing to keep your commitment, but surely you could've called to let us know you would be absent. I mean, imagine if we all just stopped being accountable, and didn't show up when we say we would, and just did whatever we want. It would be chaos, and I'm sure you don't want to contribute to chaos, do you, Megan?"

Still smiling. Him not me.

I transfer my weight from one foot to the other and try to muster the mental fortitude to defend myself, even though my mind is focused on this meeting with Fred.

"I'm fairly certain this is the first meeting I've missed, Paul. Ever. I always follow through with my commitments, except for this morning which was unavoidable. I'm sure you and the other committee members were able to have a productive meeting, despite my absence. Please forward the meeting minutes and notes to me and I'll look them over before the next meeting," I declare sternly.

I'm not in the mood to be bullied right now.

"But will you have time to read the minutes with this emergency you're dealing with? Maybe if you told me what the emergency is, I could help?"

He's not trying to be helpful; he's being nosy and condescending.

"Actually, Megan, I was hoping to speak with you alone after the meeting about a different matter. Do you have a few minutes now? Or we could meet later, as long as it's today. I'll go over the meeting minutes with you and we can talk about the other thing."

"Today isn't good for me, Paul. You can email the minutes to me along with whatever else you want to discuss."

I sneak a peek at my phone and see it's almost noon. We need to get to Artsy Tartsy.

"Just fifteen minutes later today?" he implores.

He won't let this go.

"Paul, we're in a hurry." April holds her right hand up between Paul and me with her palm facing Paul in a stop position. "She told you why she missed the meeting, she apologized, now let it go. Email the meeting notes to her and if she has any questions, she'll call you." As April finishes speaking, she grabs my hand and starts walking fast up the boardwalk toward the bakery and away from Paul, dragging me along behind her like an annoyed mother pulling a defiant toddler away from the toy aisle in a store.

Her long legs take wider strides than mine, so I do a kind of shuffle-walk-jog to catch up with her.

"Thank you," I say, giving April's hand a squeeze.

She squeezes my hand in return, looks down at me, and winks.

"The only way to deal with bullies is to stand up to them," she states firmly. In a softer voice she adds, "You're going to be OK, you know. You and Hannah always have T and me, and whatever happens today with this Fred person, we've got your back."

We're more than friends, we're family.

CHAPTER 3

WHEN WE OPEN the door to Artsy Tartsy, the intoxicating and soothing aroma of freshly baked pastries and bread envelop me like a hug. I inhale deeply, letting the comforting smell fill me with warmth.

I smile and wave to Tamara who is serving a customer from behind the long, glass counter. Tamara smiles and waves back. Then without turning her head, she raises her eyebrows and moves her eyeballs to the left toward a man who is sitting alone at one of the bistro tables, focused on his phone screen.

April wishes me luck under her breath and hovers a few steps behind me as I approach his table.

"Fred?"

I instinctively extend my right hand for him to shake. He looks up at me from his phone.

"Megan?"

We shake hands.

"The owners have offered us the use of the office so we can speak privately," I say.

I gesture toward the back of the bakery and Fred stands up and follows me to the office with April following us.

The office is a small, windowless room with a simple white desk, two chairs, and a low profile, white filing cabinet. The walls, floor, and ceiling are also white, which makes the room feel less small and dark. There are accents of teal on the upholstery and teal office supplies. Photos of April, Tamara, and their two kids also dot the white walls in teal frames.

I intentionally choose the chair closest to the door, leaving Fred no choice but to sit in the other chair.

He's tall and thin, with a wiry physique, light brown hair, a receding hairline, and glasses. I'd guess he's in his early thirties. He's dressed casually in jeans, a leather belt with a large, metal buckle, running shoes, and a button-down plaid shirt. He wears a plain gold wedding band.

Standing in the doorway, April asks us if we'd like anything to drink. Fred declines, and I tell her I would like a glass of water, partly because I'm thirsty, and partly because I want her to have a reason to come back in a few minutes to check in. She closes the door behind her when she leaves.

Fred unlocks the screen on his phone and shows me more screenshots of alleged text conversations between his wife, Stephanie, and Adam. I'm about to ask him how I can verify the texts are real when he swipes the screen and shows me an intimate, revealing photo of Adam.

Despite the photo being headless, I know it's Adam. This photo would be more difficult to fake than a screenshot of a text conversation.

I'm in shock and while I'm momentarily speechless, Fred scrolls through a few more intimate photos of Adam, and explains he learned about the affair two days ago when Stephanie accidentally sent him a photo of Adam instead of a photo of their cat sitting in a cardboard box.

He says he confronted her, and she told him everything and let him look through her phone. Fred then texted the photos to me, along with the screenshots of the text conversations.

How could Adam be so stupid! I can't count the number of times we sat down with Hannah and warned her about the dangers of sending photos to people on the internet because you never know when those photos can come back to haunt you. Yet here he is, sending compromising photos of himself to some random woman, who has shared them with her husband, who then shared them with me. How many other people have seen these? Or, heaven forbid, have copies. Unbelievable.

A gentle knock at the door distracts me from my silent rant. April has a tray with water and a small plate of pastries to sample. She strategically stands just behind Fred where he can't see her.

"Are you OK?" She mouths silently, exaggerating her words so I can read her lips.

I smile and nod. She asks if we need anything else, then reminds us that she's just outside. She leaves and closes the door behind her.

I cross my legs and lean slightly toward Fred.

"What do you want, Fred?" I ask. "You could've sent these to me without a face-to-face meeting, so you must want something."

"We want Adam to leave the firm," he replies.

He said we. His wife, Stephanie knows he's here; they're working together. He's waiting for me to speak, but I stay silent, purse my lips, and continue to look him in the eye.

"Stephanie and I want to work it out, but that can't happen if she sees Adam at work every day," he explains. "Stephanie is a junior associate and Adam is a senior partner. It would be easier for him to find another job than it would be for her."

He takes a deep breath and adds, "Their relationship violates the firm's fraternization policy. Also, as a senior partner, Adam is in a position of authority over Stephanie and it *could* appear to the other partners that his influence as her boss coerced her into having an affair with him."

I feel anger bubbling up from deep inside me. My mouth is dry and hot and I can feel my face flushing. I take a sip of water and try to calm myself down.

I'm well aware of the firm's fraternization policy, and so is Adam since he wrote it. It simply states employees cannot date or engage in intimate, personal relationships with other employees.

Did Adam use his position as partner to coerce her into having an affair? For years, I've watched him passionately represent the victims of workplace harassment, and I've seen how disgusted he is with the perpetrators. The Adam

I know could never do this, but I guess that's what the wife always says when stories like this become public.

"Are you saying my husband forced your wife to have an intimate relationship with him?"

I'm trying to sound calm and composed, but I'm afraid I sound more accusatory, hostile, and threatened.

Fred shifts in his chair and averts his eyes to his lap, seeming suddenly uncomfortable.

"No." He shakes his head, still looking at his hands in his lap. "According to Stephanie, she made the first move, and I believe her."

He sits up, composes himself, and adds, "But that doesn't change the fact that the firm has a strict policy prohibiting employees from dating each other. Adam is technically her superior, and the firm regularly represents victims of workplace harassment, so the optics of this relationship wouldn't be good for the firm's reputation, or your husband's."

There it is. The reason he wanted to meet in person. Fred and Stephanie Murphy are using the photos and screenshots to blackmail Adam into leaving the firm. Fred is correct when he says this could damage or even end Adam's career.

It could also ruin us financially at a time when we have university expenses and are about the add the cost of a second household to our family budget. How would we explain this to Hannah?

"You said 'we want Adam to leave the firm.' Do you mean 'we' as in you and Stephanie? She knows you're here today. Are you speaking on behalf of both of you?"

"Yes." He nods. "She knows I'm here. She told me to speak to you in person so there wouldn't be any evidence or technological trail someone could follow."

That's rich. I stop myself from laughing out loud at the irony. They don't want any technological evidence, yet they're using a technological smoking gun to blackmail us. She's a lawyer for goodness' sake, an officer of the court, and she's participating in blackmail.

I believe him. I don't think the Murphys are bluffing. I believe they're prepared to follow through with their threat if Adam doesn't leave the firm.

"What EXACTLY are you asking ME to do?" I ask.

I don't want any more details or explanations. I want to find out what I need to know so I can get out of this tiny office and away from Fred Murphy, before I throw up.

"We want today to be Adam's last day at the firm. Steph called in sick yesterday and today, but she's going back to work tomorrow, and if Adam is still there, she's going straight to the partners. I spoke with Adam earlier today, and he knows what we expect. I thought you had a right to know. You're a victim, like me. You and I are collateral damage. But you might want to encourage him to do the right thing, so you and your daughter don't have to deal with the fallout if he doesn't."

"Does Adam know you've contacted me?" I ask, wondering if this is why Adam has been blowing up my phone with calls and texts all morning.

"No, he doesn't," Fred shakes his head. "I'll leave that up to you."

"I see." I stand up and put my hand on the door knob.

"I'd say it was nice to meet you, Fred, but it wasn't. Enjoy the rest of your day."

Fred stands up and I step out of the office and into the bakery so he can walk past me and leave. I pick up the water and plate of pastries, follow him to the front of the bakery, and watch him leave.

The bakery is empty except for me, April, and Tamara who comes out from behind the counter and locks the door behind Fred. She turns the OPEN sign to CLOSED and comes back to where I'm standing at the counter and wraps her arms around me. Feeling safe now that Fred has left, I start to cry.

I tell April and Tamara about my conversation with Fred, compose myself, dry my tears, and thank them for letting me use the office and always having my back.

It's almost time for me to start my shift at Knitorious, and I need to tell Connie about everything that's happened today.

After a group hug, I turn to leave. Tamara accompanies me to the door, and as she unlocks it she makes a joke about flipping the CLOSED sign to OPEN before Paul Sinclair hears Artsy Tartsy is closed and comes rushing over to recite and enforce the many bylaws that are probably violated when a Water Street business closes in the middle of a business day. We chuckle and I step into the warmth of the midday sun.

So much has happened today. It's not even 1 p.m., and it already feels like the longest day of my life.

I turn left and start walking toward Knitorious. I reach

into my tote bag and retrieve my phone. Adam phoned and texted again while I was meeting with Fred.

I'm trying to work out what to say to Adam, when I notice Paul Sinclair and Fred Murphy sitting in a car together in front of a parking meter having an animated discussion. Two people who've both tried to bully me today are sitting together and shouting at each other.

I lower my sunglasses from the top of my head to my eyes to hide my gaze and slow my pace as I pass the car in an effort to hear what they're saying. I can't hear them, but it looks like they're both speaking at the same time, and their facial expressions and hand gestures indicate they're arguing.

This is a stark contrast to the soft-spoken, calm Fred I just met at the bakery, and to the cool, composed wolf-like Paul that I'm used to seeing around town.

What would they be arguing about? Maybe Fred parked wrong, or didn't put enough money in the meter, or violated a bylaw, and Paul is reprimanding him. I'm so distracted thinking about their heated discussion that I almost walk right past Knitorious.

CHAPTER 4

I OPEN the door and listen for one of my favourite sounds, the familiar jingle of the bell over the door. Other than home, Knitorious is the only place that makes me feel both relaxed and inspired at the same time.

The store is spacious with dark wood floors and yarn-filled, white shelving along the walls. The counter is in the centre of the store. Behind it there is a long wooden harvest-style table with ten chairs where we teach classes and sometimes sit for knit night. In front of the counter, and off to the side, there are two sofas, two overstuffed chairs, and a coffee table arranged in an intimate, cozy sitting area for knitting. As far as yarn stores go, Knitorious is classic yet contemporary, just like Connie, the owner.

I spot Connie at the winding station, a small wooden table with a yarn swift and ball winder attached to it. A yarn swift is a wooden contraption that holds a skein of yarn while it's being wound into a ball. We wrap the skein of yarn around the yarn swift, then attach one end of the yarn to the ball winder. We crank the ball winder so the swift spins and pulls the yarn from the skein to the ball that's being wound. Aside from knitting itself, winding yarn is one of the most meditative knitting activities there is, at least in my opinion.

I start walking toward Connie, but I'm stopped at the Harvest table by Harlow, Connie's cat. He's lounging on the tabletop and exposing his belly for rubs. He purrs loudly as soon as I touch his soft, warm tummy.

"It's been a heck of a day so far!" I declare to Connie.

I'm eager to fill her in on the events of this morning, but she turns, raises her left index finger to her closed lips in a shushing gesture, then bends her finger to point to her right. I look in the direction she's pointing and see Kelly Sinclair browsing in the bulky yarn section. I nod to Connie. Message received, we aren't alone in the store.

I stash my tote bag under the counter and admire the ice-blue bulky yarn that's sitting on the counter.

"This is beautiful," I say while petting and squishing the yarn. "Is it new?"

The yarn tag says it's a bulky weight, merino-cashmere blend, and the colour is called "Breathless."

Kelly turns from the shelf of yarn where she's browsing and walks toward me.

"Isn't it gorgeous?! These skeins are going to be a new wrap for my sister. She's always complaining it's freezing in her office, and this colour is perfect for her!"

She joins me with her perfectly manicured hands in petting and squishing the skeins of yarn.

Kelly owns and operates Hairway to Heaven. She's married to Paul Sinclair, and they live in the apartment above the salon. Kelly is nothing like her husband. Kelly is pleasant, lovely to talk to, and genuinely nice. She's not imposing or prone to bullying like Paul.

She's one of the most glamorous women in Harmony Lake. Her long, blonde hair is always perfectly blown out so it's smooth and bouncy, her make-up is always applied with professional precision, her nails are perpetually manicured, she wears classic, elegant clothes, and her smile lights up a room. She's a walking testimonial to the salon's services. I sometimes wonder what she and Paul have in common. They couldn't be more different; they're living proof that opposites attract.

"Connie offered to wind one of the skeins for me," Kelly explains, "so I can cast on between clients. I doubt I'll get the chance, though, I'm fully booked for the rest of the day. And...oh....look at the time!"

Kelly checks the time on her phone, then retrieves her wallet from her purse.

"I have to get back to the salon, Mrs. Willows is coming in for roots and highlights at 2 p.m., and the plumber said he'd be over to clear the drains in the hair sinks sometime after 1:30. I should pay and get out of here before I'm distracted by more yarn!"

"Is it Archie or Ryan who's coming to unclog your drains?" I ask.

Archie and Ryan Wright are Harmony Lake's local father-son handyman service. Most of the businesses on Water Street, and residents in the rest of the town, call them for handy work and repair jobs. Their white van with the words, The Wright Men For The Job, painted on the sides in red letters, is a common sight in and around Harmony Lake.

"We don't hire Archie and Ryan anymore." Kelly's smile disappears, and is replaced with a solemn, serious expression. "Paul says Ryan isn't trustworthy, and he doesn't want him in the salon or the apartment ever again."

"Oh. Did Paul say why?"

I've never heard anyone complain about either Archie or Ryan.

"No, just that he doesn't trust him and doesn't want me to hire him." She shrugs and pulls her credit card from her wallet.

Connie stops winding and grabs a pair of large knitting needles from the needle display. The 15 millimetre wooden needles look more like drum sticks than knitting needles. But big needles are needed for bulky yarn.

"If you don't get gauge with these, Kelly, just bring them back, and we'll exchange them for a different size."

Connie hands me the needles and I ring them up. Kelly pays, I put her yarn and needles in a paper bag with handles, and she rushes out the door to beat Mrs. Willows and the plumber to Hairway to Heaven.

"What do you think that's all about? Paul not trusting Ryan?" I ask Connie now that we're alone.

Connie waves her hand in front of her face as though waving away a bad smell. "Who knows? Paul is always picking on someone, and if he's not picking on them today, he's looking for a reason to pick on them tomorrow. You know how he is, I'm sure it's something from nothing."

I reach under the counter and grab my knitting bag from my tote bag.

I've been carrying this purple yarn around for a week waiting for the chance to cast on a new hat and cowl for Hannah.

I take my knitting to one of the sofas and settle in to knit while I tell Connie about the texts from Fred, the encounter April and I had with Paul Sinclair, my meeting with Fred, the blackmail scheme, and the weird argument I saw between Fred and Paul on my way to work. I'm trying to knit while I talk, but Harlow decides that napping on my lap is more comfortable than napping on the table, so I put my knitting aside to stroke the purring, sleepy, cat.

Connie is a great listener and often a source of sage advice. I know she worries about Hannah and me, especially with Adam and I separating. I don't want to make her worry any more than she already does, but not telling her would feel like lying. I tell her and April almost everything. She even introduces me to people as her daughter-friend, and I call her my mother-friend.

Despite being only sixty-eight years young, Connie is smart, sophisticated, and wise in the ways of the world; yet, the concept of sending intimate text messages seems to elude her. She keeps asking how I can be certain it's Adam in the photos if his face isn't in any of them.

Without being explicit, I assure her it's definitely him in the photos. She's worried the photos are fake, and we're being conned, so she asks to see them for herself. Obviously, that can't happen, so to stop this conversation from becoming more awkward, I tell her I know it's Adam because his tattoo is in some of the photos. Thankfully, she accepts this and stops asking. I quickly change the subject, and we discuss ideas for the fall window display.

I'm pretty sure this isn't a lie. I think I recall seeing his tattoo featured in one of the photos, but I'm not certain because I haven't looked at them since Fred sent them to me. In fact, I'd like it very much to never see them again. Adam has Hannah's birth date tattooed in roman numerals over his heart.

When Connie gets up to answer the phone, I pick up my phone to see more notifications of calls and texts from Adam.

I have to tell him that I know, but I'm at a loss for words so I send him one of the screenshots of a text conversation between him and Stephanie. I'm careful to send him the least-intimate thing that Fred sent me. As soon as I hit send, I see three dots on the screen and know Adam is typing a reply.

Adam: I'm sorry. This will be taken care of today. You spoke to Paul?

What does *taken care of* mean? Does that mean he's going to leave the firm, or does it mean something else? And how does he know Paul was looking for me? I miss one meeting in sixteen years and Paul calls my husband? Seems like a bit of an overreaction on Paul's part, but OK.

Me: Yes, he found me on my way into town.

I want to tell him about my meeting with Fred, but I'm

a bit paranoid about putting it in a text since I've now got a phone full of incriminating photos and screenshots of text conversations. I hit send and no dots appear. Instead my phone rings and it's Adam's number on the call display.

"Hi," I whisper, aware Connie is on the phone in the kitchenette in back of the store.

I stretch to look through the doorway and see her back is to me, her sleek, shoulder-length grey hair bobbing around as she talks on the phone.

Connie is an animated talker. She uses her hands and facial expressions to add emphasis when she speaks. If people were books, most of us would be novels, but Connie would have full colour illustrations. She uses gestures to add context to what she's saying.

"Meg, I'm so sorry. I didn't know any of this would happen."

"Which part didn't you know, Adam? That your girlfriend is married? That dating an employee is against the company policy that *you* wrote? That you're technically her boss? That those photos could be used against us? That sleeping with an employee might hurt your career? That I might see a bunch of photos I wish I didn't know exist? You'll need to be more specific, Adam."

There's a long angry silence. Well, angry for me. For Adam it might be an awkward silence.

"I know I messed up, Meg, and I'm fixing it. I've been in meetings with the other partners for most of the day, and I'll be here late tonight taking care of it. If you're still awake when I get home, I'd like us to talk, so I can explain some things to you. If it's too late tonight, maybe we can talk tomorrow."

He's telling me he'll be late like it's a rare occurrence, like he hasn't been working late and bringing work home with him on weekends for the better part of fifteen years. We do need to talk about this, though, he's right about that.

"Fine," I agree. "Let's talk either tonight or tomorrow."

Just as I'm about to ask him what "taking care of it" means, I'm interrupted by the jingle of the bell over the door. A local yarn dyer is struggling to hold the door open while carrying a tub of yarn that Connie must have ordered. I tell Adam I have to go, end the call, and rush to hold the door for the dyer.

In between serving customers, helping a knitter recover a stitch she dropped about three hundred rows ago, and petting Harlow on demand, I unpack the tub of yarn, add the skeins to the store inventory, take photos of them for the shopping section of the store website, and rearrange some shelves to make room for the new, fall-coloured skeins.

Harlow and I both look up when we hear the clinking sound of dishes. Harlow's pupils dilate, his tail is twitchy and his ears are at attention. He's on full alert. The *ffffffffpp* sound of the lid being pulled off a can of cat food confirms his suspicion; his dinner is almost ready. He runs to the back of the store, and into the kitchenette where I hear the *tinking* sound of the spoon tapping his plate as Connie doles out the gross-smelling loaf of cat food onto his dish.

How is it dinner time already? A quick glance at the

clock on the cash register tells me it's twenty minutes past six. We should have closed twenty minutes ago. I go to lock the door and turn the sign to CLOSED, but the door is already locked and the sign is already turned.

"I closed up twenty minutes ago, my dear." Connie is out of the kitchenette and sitting at the harvest table. "You were so focused on what you were doing that you didn't notice."

"I was focused on keeping myself busy, so I wouldn't have time to think about Murphygate. It didn't work."

I credit April for coming up with the name, Murphygate. She used it a couple of hours ago when she texted me for an update.

"Have you heard anything more from Adam or the Murphygate people, my dear?"

Hearing Connie say the phrase, Murphygate people, makes me smile.

"You know I would tell you if I did. I'm hoping no news is good news, and I'll never hear from them again."

"You should stay for supper tonight. We'll make tacos and drink wine. We can watch that British murder mystery show you like and have a sleepover! We haven't had a girls' night in ages." Connie claps her hands together in front of her chest as if she's just come up with the best idea ever.

Connie dotes on me. I know she's choosing tonight for a girls' night to help keep my mind off Murphygate, and so she can stay close if there's another dramatic development.

"I'd love a girls' night, but can we do it another night?

Today has been exhausting and I think I'd fall asleep before I finish my tacos and wine."

I'm moving around the store, picking up mislaid skeins of yarn, and returning them to the proper shelves when I notice the half-wound skein of "Breathless" yarn at the winding station.

"Kelly paid for that skein but was in a rush to get back to the salon and left without it," I say to Connie, while nodding toward the winding station behind her.

"Oh mothballs! I completely forgot to finish winding it." Connie turns her chair around and starts cranking the ball winder.

I tidy the store while Connie finishes winding the skein of yarn.

"I can drop it off to her on my way home," I offer. "I have to walk past the salon anyway."

I place the ball of yarn in a small bag and drop the bag in my tote. Connie follows me to the door so she can lock it behind me.

"I'll see you in the morning." I open my arms for a hug.

Connie squeezes me and rubs my back.

"Call me tonight if you need anything." She pulls away and points at my nose. "I mean it. I don't care how late it is."

"I will, I promise! Goodnight."

I open the door, listening for the jingle, step onto the sidewalk, and hear the door lock behind me as I start to walk down the street.

CHAPTER 5

I'M ABOUT to turn up the alleyway next to the salon that will take me to the back door that leads to the upstairs apartment, when I notice the lights are still on inside the salon, so I go to the salon door instead.

I reach for the door handle and read the business hours posted on the door. The salon closes at 6 p.m. on Tuesdays, and It's almost 7 p.m. now. I pull the door but it's locked. I try pushing it anyway, because I've made that mistake before, and determine the door is definitely locked.

I bring my right hand to my forehead to reduce the glare of twilight reflecting off the salon window, and squint, looking inside.

I see the back of Kelly's head. She's standing at one of the sinks with a client. I pull the bag of yarn from my tote bag and knock on the window. When Kelly turns and sees me, I wave, smile, and hold up the bag, so she can see it. She turns back to her client, then turns back to me and walks toward the door, smiling, and wiping her hands on a black towel with a pink, embroidered salon logo on it. Kelly opens the door and I step inside.

"One of your lovely skeins of yarn was accidentally left on the ball winder," I tell her.

The chemical smell inside the salon burns my nose and throat. I wonder if Kelly is ever bothered by the fumes, or if she's used to it. I hand Kelly the bag, and she looks inside.

"Thank you for dropping it off. I've been too busy to notice it's missing. I don't usually work this late, but Mrs. Pearson and her husband are leaving for a cruise tomorrow to celebrate their forty-fifth wedding anniversary, and this was the only time I could fit her in before she leaves."

Kelly looks toward Mrs. Pearson who is waiting in a semi-reclined position with her head in the sink. "We want to make sure your hair looks sun-kissed in your vacation photos, don't we Mrs. Pearson?" Kelly asks in a raised voice so Mrs. Pearson can hear her from inside the sink.

Mrs. Pearson raises a freshly manicured thumb in acknowledgement.

Still looking toward Mrs. Pearson and holding the yarn bag up high enough for Mrs. Pearson to see, Kelly says loudly, "I'll be right back to finish taking out your foils, Mrs. Pearson, I just need to run this upstairs to the apartment."

Mrs. Pearson again raises her thumb in acknowledgement. Kelly turns to me and wrinkles her nose.

"I don't want to leave it in the salon where it can

absorb the chemical odours," she explains, her voice back to its normal volume.

"I can take it upstairs for you," I offer. "You finish getting Mrs. Pearson's hair cruise-ready, and I'll take the yarn up to your apartment."

I smile and take the bag from Kelly's hand.

"Thanks Megan, you're a star. Paul is probably at a meeting somewhere, but if he's up there, just give him the bag. If he's not, the rest of the yarn is on a table just inside the door. The door should be unlocked."

By the time she finishes speaking, she's already back at the sink with her fingers in Mrs. Pearson's hair, and I can hear the crunching sound of the foil strips Kelly is removing from her hair.

I walk to the back of the salon and turn on the light in the small back room. This back room is smaller than the back room at Knitorious and has towels, bottles of shampoo, conditioner and other salon products neatly organized on floor-to-ceiling shelves along two walls. The back door that leads to the parking lot is directly in front of me and is propped slightly ajar with a unique, heart-shaped grey rock. I assume Kelly opens it to let fresh air into the salon to combat the chemical smell. The stairs that lead up to the apartment are on my left.

From the top of the stairs I can hear a TV or radio from inside the apartment, so I assume Paul is home. I'm not looking forward to ending my day with another conversation with him.

I knock on the door hoping I'm not about to be greeted with a reprimand, lecture, or any other lengthy conversation. I can feel my stomach rumbling, and I'm thinking about the leftover lasagna waiting for me at home in the fridge. I can be at home and have it in the microwave within ten minutes of leaving here.

He doesn't answer my knock, so I knock again, louder. Still nothing. I put my ear to the door. There's definitely a TV or radio on, but I don't hear any other sounds. Maybe he went out and left the TV on? Or maybe he's asleep?

I tentatively turn the doorknob to confirm the door is unlocked. It is. I open the door slowly, just enough to poke my head inside the apartment.

"Hello? Paul? It's Megan. I'm just dropping off some yarn for Kelly," I call out.

I wait a few seconds. No response. I feel a sense of chilly apprehension about walking into the apartment, but I brace myself and go over my plan. I'll open the door, step inside, and put the yarn on the table where the other yarn is sitting. Then I'll leave and tell Kelly on my way out that Paul didn't answer, so I left the yarn on the table.

Deep breath.

I open the door slowly and step inside the apartment, and just like Kelly said, there's a small table next to the door on the right. The top of the table has a bowl of keys, two pairs of sunglasses, a wallet, and the paper bag I handed to Kelly at Knitorious this afternoon. I place the new bag of yarn on the table next to the other bag of yarn, feeling relieved I've avoided another possibly unpleasant, confrontation with Paul.

I turn to my left to leave and see Paul sitting at the kitchen table with his back to me. He's slumped forward, and I can't see his head. I assume it's on the kitchen table. What an odd place to fall asleep.

"Hi Paul." I watch him to see if he wakes up, or twitches, or something. He doesn't.

I hesitantly take a step toward the kitchen table.

"Paul?"

No response, no movement.

Ignoring the rapidly growing apprehension I feel, I continue carefully toward the kitchen table. I stop when I feel my knot. I get a familiar knot in my stomach when something isn't right. It's one of the voices my intuition uses to communicate with me. In almost forty years, the knot hasn't been wrong yet.

Now that I'm closer, I can see something blue around Paul's neck. I squint in case my eyes are playing tricks on me. Is that a skein of yarn? Why would he have a skein of yarn draped around his neck? I recognize the yarn immediately; it's a skein of "Breathless," the same yarn I admired at work today, and the same yarn that Kelly bought four skeins of today.

The skein is untwisted and wrapped around Paul's neck like a back-drop necklace, tight in the front with the excess yarn draped down the back of the white undershirt he's wearing.

I bend over to look at his face, except I can't see his face because it's immersed in a large bowl. I check for signs of life. He's eerily still, and his body isn't rising and falling like a body does when it inhales and exhales.

"Paul, I'm going to check your pulse," I tell him.

It's been more than a dozen years since I've had any

CPR training, but I remember the instructor saying it's important to talk to the patient and tell them what you're doing each step of the way.

His hands are flat on the table, palms down, on either side of the bowl that contains his head. His cell phone is next to his left hand.

I check his wrist for a pulse. No pulse. His skin feels warmer than room temperature, but not as warm as it should be.

Maybe this just happened and there's still time to help him.

"Paul, can you hear me? I'm going to lift your head out of the bowl."

I hope he can hear me.

I hope he's had some kind of bizarre household accident or medical episode but will be all right.

I put one hand on either side of Paul's head, just above his ears and lift his head from the bowl. It's heavier than I expect, and milk drips from his face into the bowl and onto the table. There are pieces of soggy cereal stuck to his nose and cheek.

He's not going to be all right.

Paul is dead.

CHAPTER 6

I INHALE SHARPLY. The knot in my stomach has turned to panic and is emanating from my gut into the rest of my body. My heart is thumping in my ears, and I can feel my face flushing. I have to get help. I have to get out of here.

Should I put his face back in the cereal bowl? Do I move the cereal bowl out of the way and put his head on the table? The CPR course didn't cover this.

How can he be dead? I just saw him this morning and he was alive. Controlling and bossy, but alive.

Did he drown in a giant bowl of cereal? Was he strangled by the skein of yarn?

I turn his head to the left so his nose and mouth won't be submerged again and gently place his head on the bowl. I'm walking backwards to the door, watching him in case I'm wrong, and he moves.

Please move! Please wake up, Paul!

I grope for the doorknob behind me and back out of the apartment.

Running down the stairs to the salon, I hear myself scream.

"Kelly! Kelly! Call 9-1-1! Something's wrong with Paul!"

Kelly looks at me with a confused look on her face.

My phone is in my shaky hand and I call for help.

While I'm answering the dispatcher's questions, Kelly is looking from me to the back of the store where the stairs are, then back to me again. I sense she's about to run up to the apartment. Should I spare her from seeing her husband like this? What if it's a crime scene? I position myself between Kelly and the stairs while continuing to answer the dispatcher's questions. Kelly wipes her hands on a towel, then sprints from sink to the back room. She pushes past me and tears up the stairs.

"Paul!" She screams.

I run up the stairs after her. She's kneeling at his side checking for a pulse. She's checking the same wrist I checked moments before, and I hope she has a different outcome.

When the dispatcher asks me to make sure the salon door is open, I run back downstairs and past the back door. I tell her it's propped open with a rock. I keep running to the front door and turn the latch to unlock it, then I push it open about an inch to confirm it's unlocked.

I hear the crinkling sound of aluminum foil and turn to see Mrs. Pearson on her feet, removing the last of the foils from her hair. She bends forward into the sink and gives her short hair a quick rinse, then while rubbing her wet hair with a towel, walks over to me and tells me that she'll take over door duty. I nod in response.

I walk to the back door in case the ambulance pulls into the parking lot behind the salon instead of out front. I'm still holding the phone up to my ear, but aside from the dispatcher saying, "Are you still with me, Megan?" every few seconds, and me responding, "Yes, I'm here," we aren't saying anything.

An ambulance pulls up in front of the Hairway To Heaven, and its lights create a red and blue strobe effect on the walls inside the salon. The dispatcher and I end our call.

Within what feels like seconds, the salon is full of first responders. Paramedics, police officers, and a few firefighters rush around me.

The back room is small, so I step into the salon and lean against the nearest wall to stay out of the way of the those who need to access the stairs.

A police officer leads Kelly down the stairs, slowly.

I go into the kitchenette and get her a glass of water. At least I'm doing something. I need to do something useful. Anything.

The officer leads Kelly to a chair in front of one of the sinks and helps her sit down. I hand Kelly the water and place a box of tissues I found on the counter in the kitchenette on her lap.

A second police officer guides me away from Kelly and over to one of the stylist's chairs on the other side of the salon.

I notice a third police officer with Mrs. Pearson at the reception desk.

We're obviously being kept apart on purpose.

One of the things I've learned from many years of binge-watching murder mysteries and true crime documentaries while I knit, is that witnesses at a crime scene are kept apart so they can be interviewed separately without influencing each other's statements.

People are highly suggestible, particularly when they're in shock, and their recollection of events can be influenced by other people's recollection of events. For example, if I think something at the crime scene is blue, but I hear another witness describe it as green, it might alter my recollection, causing me to believe the thing I saw was actually green.

My police officer opens her notepad and starts asking me questions. I fiddle with my wedding ring, now on my right hand, and provide her with my name and contact information. Then I reach into my tote bag for my wallet so I can show her my identification.

Inside my head, Adam's voice is telling me not to answer any more questions without a lawyer, but I know I haven't done anything wrong and I have nothing to hide, so I decide to cooperate, answer her questions, and help any way I can.

She asks me why I'm at the salon and why I went upstairs. She also wants to know how I found Paul, where I touched him, and what else I touched while I was up there. I tell her everything starting from the moment when

Connie and I noticed the skein of yarn that Kelly left behind at Knitorious earlier today.

The firefighters seem to have left, but more people arrive to take their place, including a tall official-looking man in a suit.

My police officer and I both notice the suit at the same time, and she excuses herself to speak with him. My experience as an avid viewer of murder mysteries tells me the man wearing the suit is a police detective.

Like a mantra, I've been repeatedly telling myself that Paul had a medical episode, or an accident, and he wasn't murdered. I don't want to believe one of my neighbours could be a murder victim and a murder could happen in this cozy, sweet town. However, the arrival of a detective makes it difficult to keep fooling myself that either my medical episode theory or accident theory are how Paul died.

If Paul's death is a murder, I was at a murder scene probably mere moments after the killer fled. This realization makes me feel anxious and leaves a sick taste in my mouth.

Suddenly, I'm hot, my breathing is shallow, I'm trembling, and my mouth is uncomfortably dry. I try taking deep breaths to control the trembling, but the chemical smell in the salon is working against me, so now I'm also nauseous. I close my eyes and put my head between my knees.

"Are you all right?" asks an unfamiliar man's voice.

I raise my head to see the suit standing in front of me.

"Would it be possible for me to step outside for some

fresh air?" I gulp, hoping to swallow the wave of nausea washing over me.

"Of course," he replies, "follow me."

He extends a hand to help me up, leads me to the front door and onto the sidewalk where I inhale as much of the crisp, evening air as my lungs can handle.

"Heavy shoulders, long arms," I mutter to myself.

"Heavy shoulders, long arms" is a relaxation technique to help release the tension from the neck and shoulders. I learned it in a yoga class in my twenties, and still use it all these years later.

"Pardon?" the suit asks. "Did you say something?"

I shake my head and lean against the cool brick wall of the salon, put my hands on my knees and take a few more deep breaths.

Feeling slightly less nauseous and shaky, I stand upright and see the sidewalk across the street lined with friends and neighbours. There are police officers and barriers preventing them from coming closer.

A uniformed officer comes running out and stands in front of me with a large white sheet. Is he trying to shield me from seeing the people across the street, or is he trying to shield the people across the street from seeing me? Either way it's too late.

"Someone is getting you a glass of water," the suit informs me.

I look up at him and nod.

"Thank you," I respond, "I'm feeling better. We can go back inside."

I return to the same chair I was sitting in before I left,

and Mrs. Pearson, followed closely by her police escort, hands me a glass of water and begins rubbing my back reassuringly. This woman is good in a crisis.

Just when I'm beginning to feel like this day will never end, my police officer appears at my side and asks me if there's someone I'd like to call to pick me up.

My first thought is to call either April or Connie, but it seems silly to ask them to escort me home when I can walk there myself in five minutes. Also, they'll fuss over me and ask a ton of questions I'm not sure I'm ready to answer. I'm not prepared to relive this again tonight. I'm tired and hungry, and I just want to go home and put on my pyjamas

My next thought is to call Adam. Not for emotional support, but because he's a lawyer, and if ever there was a situation where a lawyer might come in handy, this would be it.

Ultimately, I decide not to call anyone, and the police officer offers to drive me home. I accept.

WALKING THROUGH MY FRONT DOOR, I feel like a weight has been lifted off my shoulders. Five minutes ago, I was exhausted and overwhelmed, and now I'm wide awake and wired. This must be what it feels like to be in shock. Tonight, I've learned that being in shock is a process with a wide spectrum of reactions ranging from panic, fear, sadness, and nausea, to energetic, hyper, alert, and overwhelmed.

Vaguely, I recall once reading something about adrenaline and stressful situations, but I can't remember the details.

Adam isn't home yet, and I'm relieved I don't have to answer any questions about what happened or be reminded about the importance of not answering police questions without a lawyer.

I put a piece of lasagna in the microwave and while it warms up, I retrieve my phone from my bag and unlock the screen to see dozens of texts from friends and neighbours wanting to know what's happening, and if everyone is OK.

I reply to April and Connie immediately, letting them know Kelly, Mrs. Pearson, and I are OK, but Paul isn't. I also tell them that I need a few hours to process everything, and I'll talk to them tomorrow. They both offer to come over and not ask any questions. I appreciate it, but I thank them and decline. Right now, I'm content to be on my own, and finally let this day end.

Scrolling through the rest of the messages, I see Adam texted earlier in the evening to say I shouldn't wait up, and he'll be around in the morning to talk.

I text him back and tell him that Paul has been found dead and the town is in shock. He's going to find out anyway, and it may as well be from me. I don't tell him that I was the one who found him or that it might be murder.

He doesn't respond.

It's much later than I would normally eat dinner, but I haven't eaten since this morning, and I'm both starving and nauseous at the same time. As a result, I eat my lasagna faster than I should, hoping I won't be up all night with indigestion as a result.

I put my dishes in the dishwasher and make a mug of chamomile tea while I finish scrolling through the missed text messages.

I lay in bed tossing and turning, tired and wide awake at the same time. When I close my eyes and try to be still, I relive it all over again. I see Paul hunched over the table. I see Kelly sprinting for the stairs. I smell the chemical odour in the salon, I see milk dripping off his nose and the pieces of cereal stuck to his face. I feel his not-quite-warm-enough skin. It plays over and over in my head like a movie I can't pause.

To distract myself, I turn on the TV and find a channel that only airs 1990s sitcoms and leave it on in the background until I either fall asleep, or it's time to get up.

With the theme song from Friends filling my bedroom, I close my eyes and take deep breaths.

CHAPTER 7

WEDNESDAY, September 11th

I wake up to the voices of Paul and Jamie Buchman arguing about a pretty nurse on Mad About You. I know I slept for a little while because I dreamt I was running around the edge of a huge fountain of cereal, trying not to fall in while being chased by a giant skein of yarn.

I turn off the TV, hurry through my morning routine, and rush out the door to Knitorious.

Adam's car isn't in the driveway, and his briefcase, shoes, and coat aren't where they usually are when he's home, so I assume he hasn't been home yet.

I decide to walk into town because the police could still have Water Street closed in front of Hairway to Heaven, and I think I'm too tired to drive.

As soon as I turn the corner onto Water Street, I see the yellow crime scene tape glistening in the light of the dawning sun and wafting gently in the breeze blowing off the lake. I cross the street because the police officer stationed in front of Hairway To Heaven probably won't let me walk on the sidewalk in front of the salon.

There aren't as many bystanders this morning as there were last night, but still a good-sized crowd. As I thread my way through clusters of onlookers, I hear my name. I stretch my neck to look above the crowd and see April waving me over to where she and Connie are standing.

We have a group hug.

"How did you sleep, my dear?" Connie squeezes my shoulder with one arm and hands me a coffee with the other.

"Thank you!" I immediately hold it under my nose and inhale its glorious aroma. The first sip tells me it's a hazelnut-French vanilla medium roast, and right now, it's the best coffee in the world.

April leans in and speaks quietly in my ear, "Phillip was here really early to receive a flower delivery, and he said he saw Kelly, wrapped in an afghan, get into the back of a police car and be driven away."

Phillip Wilde is the florist who owns Wilde Flowers which is next to Knitorious, and he also lives next door to me. We're neighbours at work and at home.

"Poor Kelly," I say.

I thought my night was bad. I can't imagine what she's going through.

People start to notice me in the crowd and come over to ask how I'm doing. Some people are sincerely concerned, some are not-so-subtly trying to find out what I know, and some fall into both categories.

In light of all the attention, Connie suggests we make our way to Knitorious, and we start walking away from the other onlookers.

I'm not sure what I should say and what I shouldn't. On one hand, I want to respect Kelly's privacy and the police investigation, but on the other hand, I understand this is a small, tight-knit community and a tragedy like this affects everyone who lives and works here.

After we've put some distance between us and the crowd, April asks if anyone official has declared that Paul was murdered and if this is a murder investigation.

"I don't know," I reply. "I answered a lot of questions last night, but I didn't ask any. It didn't look like he passed away peacefully in his sleep, but it also didn't look like a gruesome murder scene."

This is the most I've said to anyone other than the police officer who questioned me.

"Not all murders are gruesome, my dear. Look at those murder mystery shows set in quaint British villages, they're never messy."

Connie shares my enthusiasm for murder mysteries. We're both experienced armchair murder investigators.

ONCE WE'RE inside the store, I lock the door behind us. The store doesn't open for another two hours, and I'm not ready to deal with more people yet.

Connie excuses herself and goes up to her apartment for a shower, while April and I sit in the cozy sitting area finishing our coffees. Harlow runs down the stairs and nestles into April's hip beside her on the sofa, settling in for his early morning nap.

"I know Paul was a bully and rubbed a lot of people the wrong way, but someone would have to hate him an awful lot to kill him. Especially in his own home with his wife in the same building," April speculates, while absentmindedly stroking Harlow. "I mean, they risked being seen by Kelly unless they entered the apartment from the roof."

"If they were already in the apartment when Paul got home, they only risked being seen when they left," I point out.

I'm fiddling with my ring, still getting use to wearing it on my right hand.

"The killer either knew Kelly would be working late in the salon and Paul would be alone in the apartment, or they intended to kill both Paul and Kelly, and since Kelly wasn't there, they had to settle for only killing Paul," she surmises.

"Yesterday when Kelly was here picking out yarn, she told Connie and me that Paul doesn't want her to hire The Wright Men For The Job anymore because he doesn't trust Ryan. He told her he doesn't want Ryan in the salon or the apartment ever again," I tell her.

"That's interesting." April nods and raises her eyebrows.

"I wonder if Mr. and Mrs. Pearson were able to leave for their cruise?"

"You mentioned her last night in your text, but we didn't see her there. I don't think anyone saw her there, and other than you, no one else has mentioned her," April says.

"She was the client Kelly stayed late for. No one else knows that?"

"No. We only knew you were there because you came outside for air. The police held up sheets to block the view when anything, or I guess anyone, came outside."

April leaves for Artsy Tartsy, so she can take over working the counter and Tamara can work her magic in the kitchen.

Now that I'm alone with my thoughts, my mind replays last night's events on a constant loop, and I worry I missed telling the police something important, or I compromised something when I found Paul and tried to help him. Maybe I shouldn't have lifted his head or put it back in a slightly different position.

Harlow wakes up and meows loudly at me.

"I know what you want, handsome. You only ever want one thing." I pick him up, carry him to the kitchenette and put him on the floor. He weaves in and out of my ankles while I spoon his breakfast onto a dish and put it on the floor in front of him.

I walk back into the store and Adam is standing outside the window waving at me. I unlock the door and let him in.

"I knocked, but I guess you didn't hear it in the back."

He's wearing a suit. He's either on his way to the office,

or on his way home from the office. We sit on the sofa, and he tells me he didn't get my text about Paul's death until this morning. I fill him in.

"You were dropping off yarn? I assumed you were there because Paul was blackmailing us. It was him who told you about Stephanie and gave you the screenshot, right?"

"No! Paul knew about you and Stephanie? How? And how did he get the photos?" I ask, shocked. "Fred Murphy gave me the photos, not Paul."

I stop to take a breath and let this news about Paul having the photos sink in.

"Paul's blackmailing us?" I ask. "Is this in addition to Fred and Stephanie blackmailing us, or are they all working together? Is there one blackmail scheme or two? I'm so confused."

Seriously, what's going on? I might need to make a list or draw a chart or something.

Adam brings his hands together in front of his chest.

"You spoke with Fred? Fred told you about Stephanie and gave you the photos?" he asks, then points to me. I nod.

"OK, Fred and Stephanie are blackmailing me to leave the firm. Paul contacted me early yesterday morning and told me to transfer a certain amount of money into his account by noon, or he would send the photos to you," Adam explains. "There's no way I was giving in to Paul's demand, and I didn't send him any money. I tried calling and texting you, but you didn't answer. Then you texted me the photo, so I assumed

Paul followed through with his threat and told you about Stephanie."

I nod again. If Paul knew about Adam's affair and had photos, that must be why he wanted to talk to me after the committee meeting yesterday.

"I have no idea how Paul got the photos," Adam adds.

"I saw Paul and Fred together yesterday," I tell him. "They were arguing in a car outside Artsy Tartsy just before 1 p.m. I assumed Fred was parked wrong, or didn't use his blinker, or some such thing, but maybe they actually know each other and were talking about blackmail."

"Meg, the texts and the photos on Paul's phone, and his text conversation with me, give us motive to kill him. The police are going to want to talk to us. Soon."

"Where were you last night?" I ask. "The police will probably want to know that, too."

I'm genuinely curious where he spent the night. I know it wasn't at home, and I assume it wasn't with his blackmailer-girlfriend, Stephanie.

"I stayed in a courtesy suite the firm retains at a hotel near the office. I resigned yesterday, effective immediately," he explains. "I stayed late updating notes on my open cases and tying up loose ends. It was late when I left, and I was too tired to drive home, so I stayed at the hotel."

Wow. He left the firm?! This is the end of an era. Under normal circumstances, this would be a monumental event, but in light of everything that's happened since yesterday, it's almost insignificant.

I want to ask him if his affair with a married woman that cost him his job, and being blackmailed twice over was worth it, but I bite my tongue. We need calm, level heads, not heated arguments and accusations.

Creaking floorboards warn us that Connie is coming downstairs. We stop talking and Adam stands up, smooths his tie, smiles broadly, and walks toward her to greet her as she enters the store.

Adam is a dangerous combination of handsome and charming, packaged in a well-tailored, expensive suit. He has a way of looking at you that makes you feel like you're the only person in his world.

Even Connie isn't immune to his charm. I see his charisma drawing her in like a moth to a flame.

Adam takes both her hands in his. They exchange cheek kisses and he compliments her perfume as they pull apart. Still holding both of her hands in his, he tells her how beautiful she looks, and she blushes like a schoolgirl. He can't help it. He doesn't know he's doing it, and he doesn't do it in a predatory way, he's being totally sincere. This is just how he is. He's oblivious to the effect he has on people, particularly women, and his naivete is part of what makes him so charming.

They're talking about Paul and how shocking his death is for the entire community. He doesn't mention Paul was blackmailing us.

After throwing a few more compliments at her, Adam leaves and Connie and I are alone in the quiet store. Except for Harlow's purring and the gentle clicking of our needles, we knit in silence until it's time to open the store.

"It's showtime." Connie smiles at me, puts her knitting on the table and gets up to unlock the door and flip the CLOSED sign to OPEN.

CHAPTER 8

WATER STREET IS BUSIER than it would be on a normal Wednesday. But this isn't a normal Wednesday. It's the day after a member of our community was killed in his home.

People stroll up and down Water Street, meandering in and out of stores and trying to make sense of what happened to Paul. They find comfort in each other's company, reassuring each other, and not being alone today.

As shocked people wander in and out of Knitorious, Harlow makes himself available to provide comfort, demand rubs, and selflessly takes on the role of self-appointed emotional support animal.

The store is busy with both knitters and non-knitters. Some of the non-knitters at least try to pretend they've developed a sudden interest in yarn and fibre arts.

Almost everyone asks me what I saw yesterday when I was at the salon. The ones who don't ask me directly hover close by when someone else does so they can hear what I say. I tell them I can't talk about it until the police tell me otherwise. Word must have gotten around that I'm not talking because by lunchtime the number of people slows down, and most of those who do come in don't ask me to recount my experience.

Connie and I take turns having lunch. When it's my turn, I go upstairs to her apartment and have a sandwich that she made for me. I don't usually take a full lunch break. I'm happy to eat something in the kitchenette in the back room and then go back to work, but today I eat my sandwich slowly and take almost a full hour to myself.

I come back from lunch and find Connie dangling a string with a shimmery pom pom toy on the end back and forth in front of Harlow.

"Are you going to be all right if I leave for my appointment, my dear?"

I completely forgot Connie has an appointment today. She mentioned it yesterday before I went to Hairway To Heaven.

"Of course!" I say, "You go. I'll be fine. Besides, Stitch-Fix is this afternoon, so I'll be busy, and the afternoon will fly by."

Stitch-Fix is a knitting clinic we host one afternoon each week where knitters bring in their knitting problems and mistakes, and Connie and I help fix them. I love the challenge.

"Only if you're sure. I don't mind rescheduling. I meant to reschedule this morning, but in all the excitement I forgot." She shrugs and chuckles at her forgetfulness.

I know how much Connie hates being late, or

rescheduling anything, especially at the last minute, so I tell her, again, that I'll be fine. She pops up to her apartment to get her purse and leaves through the back door.

For the first time since we unlocked the door this morning, the store is empty. I take this opportunity to tidy up the shelves and return mislaid skeins of yarn back where they belong.

When I find myself in the bulky yarn section, looking at the remaining skeins of "Breathless," I feel a now-familiar wave of nausea wash over me. In my mind's eye I can still see this same yarn wrapped around Paul's neck while he's hunched over the kitchen table, the yarn dangling down the back of his white undershirt like a back drop necklace. I decide to remove it from the shelf and put it somewhere out of sight.

While I'm contemplating which yarn to put in its place, the bell over the door jingles. I turn to greet the customer, and see a tall, fortyish-year-old man in a suit, standing just inside the store, looking around. He's familiar, but I can't place him. He's not our typical demographic, and if he were a customer, I'd remember him for sure.

We make eye contact and walk toward each other, meeting at the harvest table.

"Hi," I say, smiling.

"Hello, again," he replies, also smiling.

He extends a hand and offers me a business card:

Detective Sergeant Eric Sloane
Ontario Provincial Police
Nippissing Detachment

He's the suit I met at the salon last night.

"Of course. You're the detective from Hairway to Heaven! I recognized you but couldn't place you."

I extend my hand, we shake, and I gesture for him to have a seat at the harvest table.

"Why the OPP? The Harmony Lake Police Department isn't investigating this?" I ask.

The OPP is what the locals call the Ontario Provincial Police.

"Harmony Lake PD doesn't have a major crimes division, so they've asked us to assist," he explains. "Apparently there isn't enough crime in Harmony Lake to warrant a major crimes division."

"Not until yesterday," I confirm.

It's true. Compared to bigger towns and cities, Harmony Lake has a low crime rate. We have our share of speeding tickets, parking tickets, jaywalkers, the occasional drunk-in-public tourist in the summer, and a few years back there was a spate of wallet robberies at the ski resort, but nothing like murder ever happens here.

I didn't notice yesterday, but Eric Sloane smells good. And, not to be shallow, but he's kind of hot, if you're into tall men with dark hair, brown eyes with flecks of gold, and nice smiles.

Don't stare, Megan.

"How are you?" he asks. "I know yesterday was a shock, and you weren't feeling well at the salon last night. Are you feeling better now?"

"It's a shock, for sure, but I feel better today. Thank you

for asking. I've been thinking about Kelly a lot today, how is she doing?"

"She has family with her, and we're making sure she has access to all available resources to help her right now."

It's amazing how well he answered my question without actually answering my question at all.

"Well, please tell her that everyone is thinking of her and sending her lots of love and support."

I doubt he'll literally say those words to her, but hopefully he'll relay the sentiment.

"How can I help you, Detective Sergeant?"

"Please, call me Eric."

"Only if you call me Megan."

Eric pulls a small notebook and pen from his breast pocket, and I notice he has nice hands. You know, if you're into large, strong hands with clean, nicely-groomed nails.

Don't stare at his hands, Megan.

"Can you tell me about the yarn that Ms. Sinclair purchased yesterday?"

He's found a blank page in his notebook, and his pen is in his hand poised to write.

"Sure."

I back my chair away from the table, walk over to a shelf and pick up a skein of yarn identical to the ones Kelly bought for her sister's wrap. I return to my seat and place the skein on the table between us.

He asks me how many skeins she purchased, if they were all exactly the same, and if she purchased anything else while she was here. I print a copy of her receipt and give it to him, so he can see the purchase details for himself.

"Other than the yarn, did Ms. Sinclair leave anything else behind when she left yesterday?"

"Nope. Just the yarn that I returned to her in the evening."

"Are you sure she left the store with everything else, including the knitting needles?"

"Yes. I put them in the bag myself. She definitely had the needles with her when she left."

"Did she have both of them? Is it possible one of the knitting needles was left behind?"

I walk over to the needle rack and retrieve a pair of needles identical to the ones Kelly purchased. I return to my seat at the table and place the needles on the table between us, beside the skein of yarn.

"They're packaged together," I explain. "To lose one, the packaging would have to rip or be torn in two spots in a specific way to get one needle out of the package. Connie took the needles from the rack and I rang them up and put them in the bag, and there's no way one of us wouldn't have noticed the packaging if it were torn to that extent. And Connie wouldn't have them on the rack in that state, never mind sell them."

He's nodding and making notes in his notebook. I try to read his writing, but it isn't very neat. It's small, and from my vantage point, upside down. All I can make out is the date at the top of the page.

"Can you tell me about the altercation you and Ms.

Shaw had with Paul Sinclair yesterday at the park across the street?"

He looks at me closely to gauge my reaction.

"Hmmm...it wasn't an altercation." I shake my head. "It was a typical interaction with Paul. If you classify it as an altercation, then every interaction Paul has ever had is an altercation. I missed a committee meeting yesterday morning at the Animal Centre and Paul chased me through the park to reprimand me for missing it. He wouldn't let it go, so April, Ms. Shaw, told him to back off, and we left."

He makes a scratchy note in his book then looks up at me again.

"Why did you miss the meeting at the Animal Centre?"

I take a deep breath.

"My husband's girlfriend's husband texted me and asked if we could meet."

Good luck connecting those dots, Eric!

"This is a new situation. It distracted me, pretty much derailing the rest of my morning," I explain.

He's nodding and writing in his book.

Harlow jumps onto the table, nudges his head against Eric's pen, and steps onto the page Eric is writing on. Eric stops writing. He doesn't really have a choice. He gives Harlow scratches between his ears. Harlow flops onto the notebook and purrs contentedly.

"I need to ask you some more questions, Megan. Can we set up a time to meet, so I can get a full statement from you?"

"Am I a suspect?"

CHAPTER 9

IT FEELS like my heart and my stomach switch places while I wait for an answer.

"Everyone is a suspect until they're eliminated, Megan, and your statement will help to eliminate you."

Once again, he answers my question without actually answering my question. This must be a skill they teach at the police academy.

"I didn't do it," I insist. "I wouldn't hurt anybody, never mind kill them. I don't think I'd be strong enough to strangle someone, even with a skein of yarn."

Eric raises his right hand to stop me from talking.

"Hold on. Why did you say that, about the yarn? Why do you think that's how he died?"

"I'm the person who found him, remember? I saw the yarn around his neck. Also, if he'd died of natural causes, or an accident, I don't think you and I would be having this conversation. Based on what I saw, he either drowned in a giant bowl of cereal or was strangled with a skein of yarn and then fell forward into the cereal. It would be really weird to be eating cereal while wearing a yarn-necklace, and if he was, it wouldn't have been pulled tightly against the front of his throat with the rest of the skein dangling down his back. Therefore, he must've been strangled from behind, then left with his face in the bowl."

I stop incriminating myself long enough to take a breath and realize that to Eric, it must sound like I just confessed to killing Paul by strangling him with yarn and letting his face fall into his huge cereal bowl.

This is probably why Adam is so keen on people having a lawyer present when they talk to the police.

The bell above the door at the front of the store jingles, and Harlow jumps down to greet the new arrival.

Eric closes his notebook, clicks his pen, and returns them both to his breast pocket. He pushes the skein of yarn and needles aside and puts his hands palms down on the table between us.

"Can you do me a favour please and don't tell anyone else what you just told me? Can you please keep that completely to yourself?"

I nod. I'm terrified. If I wasn't a suspect before, I am now. Why didn't I stop myself from talking? What was I thinking?

"I think someone might be here for Stitch-Fix," I tell him as I back my chair away from the table, stand up, then push the chair back in.

I walk to the front of the store and encounter a knitter with a frustrated look on her face holding a partially completed blanket with a large hole in it. I greet her, smile knowingly at her blanket, invite her to have a seat at the harvest table, and tell her I'll be right back to help her with her knitting problem.

Eric is at the door, and we agree to meet tomorrow, so I can answer more of his questions. He says he'll text me in the morning to arrange a time.

After he leaves, I shudder. Paul was definitely murdered, and there's a murderer in our midst. If it were tourist season, we might be able to blame an outsider for what happened, but the summer tourist season is over and the winter tourist season hasn't begun, which means Paul was murdered by a local. One of my neighbours is a killer.

I WAVE off the last Stitch-Fix knitter, after helping her close a hole in a sweater sleeve made when she accidentally created a stitch about sixty rows ago. I feel a rumble in my tummy, and decide to get a glass of water and a snack from the kitchenette. I'm almost at the fridge when the door jingles. I poke my head into the store and see April carrying one of my favourite things, a white confectionery box with the Artsy Tartsy logo on the lid. I grab two glasses of water and join her on the sofa.

She opens the box and reveals still-warm pumpkin oatmeal cookies for us and a small container of whipped cream for Harlow.

While the three of us enjoy our treats, I tell April about my visit from Eric Sloane and my theory about the killer being local and possibly someone we know and interact with regularly.

"Isn't it usually the spouse in books and on TV?" April asks. "I mean, Kelly had access to him, and it was her yarn that killed him."

What did she just say?

"How do you know how Paul died?"

Eric asked me not to say anything about my theory that Paul was strangled from behind with the yarn Kelly bought that day.

"It was in the WSBA group chat." She shrugs and picks up another cookie. "Apparently Mort mentioned it to someone. He said he and the coroner had to remove Paul carefully to not disturb the yarn around his neck. Whoever he told mentioned it to someone in the group chat and now the entire WSBA knows."

Which means the entire town knows. The Water Street Business Association (WSBA) group chat is for members only. Connie and April are members because they own businesses on Water Street, but I'm not. The chat is used for things like announcing sales, reminders about meetings, and gossip.

Mort Ackerman is our local funeral director. He owns Mourning Glory Funeral Home in Harmony Hills.

I make a mental note to text Eric and tell him that the thing he didn't want me to tell anybody is now common knowledge, and that it wasn't me who let the yarn out of the bag, so to speak.

"She would have had to leave Mrs. Pearson long enough to go upstairs, kill Paul, come back downstairs, and compose herself. When I got there, she was her usual, friendly, laid-back self. There was no hint that she had just killed her husband," I reason.

"But she would be composed if she's a psychopath," April deduces. "Psychopaths don't lose their composure when they kill someone, and they can act like they aren't psychopaths, that's how they trick the rest of us."

April shudders, visibly. I think we both feel weirded out at the thought of being in the proximity of a psychopath and not knowing who it is.

I reach into the box, take the last cookie, and offer it to April, but she waves it away. I break it in half and hold out half the cookie to her, but she waves it off, too, so it's all mine!

"I saw Paul and Fred in a car together when I left the bakery yesterday. They were arguing. I'm not sure if they already knew each other, or if Paul caught him breaking a bylaw and confronted him."

"That's interesting..." She nods, her gaze wandering to the left.

"Paul was having an issue with Ryan, too..." I'm speaking with my mouth full because these cookies are so good, they've made me forget my manners. I raise my right index finger, swallow the cookie, and have a sip of water. "Something had to have happened between them for Paul to not trust him."

"Paul had issues with lots of people, and lots of people had issues with him. If having an issue with Paul is all it takes to get your name added to the suspect list, almost everyone in town is on the list."

She makes a good point.

"Speaking of issues with Paul," I say, "I'm pretty sure Adam and I are at the top of the suspect list."

I take a deep breath and tell her about Paul having the photos and using them to try to blackmail Adam.

Before she can react, we're interrupted by the jingle of the front door, and Connie comes sweeping in to join us.

We fill her in on our discussion until it's time to lock the door and flip the sign to CLOSED.

CHAPTER 10

As soon as I walk in the house, I text Hannah and ask her to FaceTime with me.

Adam isn't home, and I know he'd want to be here when I tell her about Paul, but April and I agreed we need to tell both Hannah and Rachael, April and Tamara's daughter, tonight about Paul's murder. We agreed to FaceTime our daughters as soon as we get to our respective homes. This way they'll both hear it from us instead of from each other, a friend in Harmony Lake, or on social media.

I hit Send on my text to Hannah, then pull Eric's business card from my wallet and fire off a text to him explaining that the information he asked me to keep to myself is all over town because of someone else. I didn't tell him it was Mort because, first, I don't know for sure it was Mort, I only know that's what April told me she read in the WSBA group chat, and second, Eric's a detective, and if he wants to know who let the yarn out of the bag, he can use his detective skills and figure it out.

Hannah FaceTimes me and I tell her about Paul. A few minutes into our conversation the doorbell rings. I look through the living room window and see Eric Sloane standing on the porch. I open the door and gesture for him to come in as I say my goodbyes and I love yous to Hannah and end our call.

"I sent you a text a little while ago," I say as I lead us into the living room.

We sit and I offer him a beverage. He declines.

"I was driving, but I read it when I pulled into your driveway. It's difficult to keep things under wraps in such a small town. It would've been ideal to keep the yarn as a hold-back, but it's all right."

"What's a hold-back?" I ask.

Eric explains that a hold-back is a piece of evidence or information from the crime scene that only the killer or someone who was present would know about. The hold-back is useful when interrogating a suspect. If they mention the hold-back, it's a good indication they were there. A hold-back can also eliminate someone who confesses to a crime they didn't commit, because according to Eric, people actually do that. If they don't mention the holdback, it's less likely they were at the crime scene when the crime occurred.

"I'm hoping to see Mr. Martel," he says.

I feel relieved, then I feel guilty for feeling relieved that Adam is about to be questioned instead of me.

"He's not here. I can text him, let him know you're here and ask when he'll be back?"

Eric nods, "Thanks, that would be great."

I text Adam and wait for a reply.

"Do you have any idea where he might be?" he asks.

This is a loaded question. I'm pretty sure Eric has figured out Adam and I aren't happily married. I mean, telling him I met with my husband's girlfriend's husband was a big clue, and so are the photos and texts between Adam and Stephanie that Paul had on his phone. I think he's looking for me to confirm it and give him some back story without coming out and asking me directly.

"We still live under the same roof, but Adam and I have been separated for months. I don't know where he is, and we don't monitor each other's comings and goings."

That's the short version.

"Was the separation triggered by the photos on Mr. Sinclair's phone?"

He's asking carefully, as if he's trying to be sensitive to the situation, which I appreciate.

"No." I shake my head. "As far as I know, the affair with Stephanie started fairly recently. I only found out about it yesterday from Fred. He and Stephanie were prepared to make the photos public if Adam didn't leave the firm. I didn't know Paul had the photos until this morning when Adam told me. I honestly didn't know when I went to the salon yesterday that Paul knew about the affair or had photos to prove it."

My phone dings.

"It's Adam. He says he's only a few minutes away."

"That's great. Thank you. Is it possible that Mr. Martel wanted to keep the affair a secret so badly that he did something drastic?"

"No!"

I answer quickly and emphatically, so Eric sees I have no hesitation about believing that Adam didn't kill Paul.

"Adam wouldn't hurt a soul. I mean, he takes spiders outside instead of killing them, and in the winter, he puts them in the garage instead of outside, so they won't freeze," I explain.

"But spiders aren't blackmailing him, Megan."

"Adam is a smart man and a lawyer," I reason. "He knows eliminating Paul wouldn't eliminate the evidence that Paul was blackmailing him. At the very least, he would've taken Paul's phone with him and disposed of it or deleted the evidence from it to slow down the investigation, but Paul's phone was on the table with the yarn, I saw it. I doubt the contents of his phone were the only motive for his murder."

"That's very observant, but what if Mr. Martel and Mrs. Sinclair were having a relationship?"

Excuse me? Did he really suggest that Adam and Kelly are having a relationship? Adam and Kelly? Do they even know each other? Adam gets his hair cut by a barber near his office in the city, and he's always at work and hardly ever in town. How many women has Adam been seeing? Oh my god, what if he sent intimate photos to her, too?!

I'm sure the look on my face is enough to tell Eric that this is the first I've heard of it.

"Are they?" I hope I said that out loud and not just in my head.

"We've found communication between them, and evidence that they've met face-to-face. What can you tell me about that?"

I shake my head. I'm searching for words, but I'm speechless. I feel like Eric just blindsided me on purpose, and it makes me feel like I can't trust him.

We both turn to look toward the door when we hear it open. Adam walks in with a laptop box under his arm. He slips his shoes off, walks past us and into the dining room where he places the box on the dining room table.

Adam greets us, then he and Eric introduce themselves to each other and shake hands.

Would Adam like to go to the police station to talk, or would he like to do it at the house and I can go out? They're both looking to me for an answer, but I'm still speechless and processing the bombshell about Adam and Kelly. All I can do is shake my head and shrug.

Adam opts for the police station and puts his shoes on. Eric joins Adam at the door and has one hand on the doorknob.

"Thank you, Megan." Eric smiles.

His smile offends me. It's like he's pleased with himself for playing head games with me. I nod to him in response.

"Lock the door behind me and don't wait up," Adam says.

He smiles and closes the door behind him. I walk over and lock it, even though we never lock the door when one of us is home.

Everything has changed so much in 24 hours.

The more I think about it, the more this doesn't feel right. Adam and Kelly having an affair? Yesterday when I heard from Fred, my instincts told me that there was some truth to what he was telling me. Today, my instincts are telling me the opposite. They're telling me if there is a relationship between Adam and Kelly, it's not an intimate one. It's too bad instincts aren't evidence.

If they are, or were, having an affair, that would give Kelly another motive to kill Paul. Maybe he found out and was going to leave her. Or, maybe she wanted to leave him to be with Adam but Paul was making that difficult. Maybe murder is less expensive and faster than divorce. Maybe Paul was blackmailing her, too.

Kelly is always so sweet and kind to me. Could she be sleeping with my husband and still act totally normal around me?

April would say, yes, she could, if she's a psychopath.

An affair with Kelly would give Adam another motive, too. Maybe Paul threatened to tell Kelly about Stephanie, his other mistress. Or maybe Paul wouldn't get out of the way for Adam and Kelly to be together.

All this what-iffing is making my head hurt. I go into the kitchen and pour myself a small glass of wine.

I hear my phone ding in the living room, and wine-in-hand, go back in there to find it. It's a text from Connie.

Connie: According to the WSBA group chat Kelly has left the police station and is staying with her sister in the city. She can't go home because the apartment and salon are crime scenes.

Why would she want to? Paul has been dead for barely twenty-four hours. The place where he was murdered would be the last place I'd want to go if I were her.

Ding! This time it's April and it's a group text to Connie and me.

April: Did you guys hear that Kelly is staying with her sister?

Connie: Yes, that poor girl! At least she has her sister!

Me: Eric and Adam just went to the police station so Adam can be questioned. Eric hinted that Adam and Kelly might be having or have had an affair.

April: ?!?!?!

Connie: Oh my!

April: Maybe he's speculating?

Connie: I was just about to say that!

Connie's exclamation points are the text-equivalent of speaking with her hands, and it makes me smile. We all text for a little while longer, then I decide to call it a day and get ready for bed.

CHAPTER 11

THURSDAY, September 12th

On my walk to work through the drizzle and fog, I stop at Latte Da and pick up two café mochas with whipped cream.

I let myself into the yarn store through the front door and turn on the computer on my way to put away my jacket and tote bag. I leave Connie's coffee on the counter in the kitchenette for her to find when she comes downstairs.

I'm only working a half-day today and I want to process and pack the online orders, so I can drop them off at the post office on my way home.

I take care of all the technology-related tasks at Knitorious because Connie says she doesn't like technology. For someone who doesn't like it, she's quite proficient at texting and social media. But if given the choice, she'd prefer to use ledger books and checklists to keep track of the accounts and manage inventory.

Administrative tasks are one of my happy places. I majored in economics and minored in accounting, and I'm happy to be in charge of the administrivia for the store.

I check the store email, print the online orders, and walk from shelf to shelf collecting the yarn and notions to fill them. I pull out tissue paper, envelopes, and plastic Ziploc bags from under the counter. The crinkling sound of the tissue paper is a beacon that lures Harlow to the Harvest table where I'm working. He loves tissue paper, so I ball-up a couple of sheets for him to play with, and toss them onto the floor, across the store. He chases them and attacks them, a safe distance from the sheets I'm using to pack the yarn; I'm sure customers would rather receive their yarn free of cat fur.

While I'm wrapping, packing, and labeling, my phone dings. It's Eric, and he wants to know what time would be convenient to meet. I decide to finish the online orders and text him later. I want to finish up and put everything away before Harlow loses interest in his tissue paper balls and decides to help me.

I'm not eager to talk to Eric right now, anyway. I'm still angry about the way he dropped the Adam-and-Kelly bombshell without any regard for my feelings and seemed proud to shock me with it.

Connie is puttering around in the kitchenette, cleaning out the fridge and checking our supplies of coffee, tea, snacks, cat food, and treats.

"What the...? Oh, my."

"Is everything all right, Connie?" I call into the

kitchenette without losing my stride packing and addressing bubble mailers.

Connie comes into the store holding a thingamajig in her hand.

"I opened the dishwasher to empty it and this"—she holds the offending thingamajig in front of her nose—"was sitting in the bottom of the tub and is probably the reason the dishes are still dirty."

"I'm sure The Wright Men can fix it. I saw Ryan driving down Water Street on my way to work. If he's still around, maybe he can fix it today, and maybe I can ask him a few questions while he's here."

"Ask him a few questions about what, my dear?"

"What Kelly said when she was here on Tuesday, about Paul not trusting Ryan and not wanting him in the salon or the store. Right now, Adam and I are pretty high up on the suspect list, and if I can find out who the real killer is, I can clear our names."

"Are you suggesting that Ryan Wright killed Paul?"

Connie sounds incredulous, and I get it. Ryan is one of the last people I'd ever suspect of murder. But on TV the killer is always the last person everyone suspects.

"Not necessarily," I say, "but maybe whatever went on between them will shed some light on what happened to Paul."

Connie picks up the landline and calls Ryan. He happens to be servicing the walk-in cooler next door at Wilde Flowers and says he can stop by to look at the dishwasher in about an hour. I finish packing orders while

Connie goes back into the kitchenette to hand-wash the dishes in the broken dishwasher.

Almost exactly one hour later, I hear a knock at the back door. I open the door and Ryan and his toolbox get straight to work assessing the dishwasher situation. I hand him the thingamajig we think is causing the problem, and Harlow and I hover around him while Connie serves the handful of customers who are milling around the store.

Harlow rubs up against Ryan's ankles while he and I talk about Paul's murder and how shocking it is. I ask him if he's heard any rumours since he's in and out of so many homes and businesses each day. He must see a lot of people and hear a lot of things.

He says he hasn't heard anything other than sympathy for Kelly. The general consensus is that it was most likely a targeted murder by someone who Paul had a disagreement with, and not a random attack or serial killer.

"Are you one of the people Paul had a disagreement with?" I ask, trying to be delicate.

He doesn't seem phased by my question and continues tightening, or possibly loosening, I can't tell the difference, the thing he's either tightening or loosening, without losing his rhythm.

"Now, why would you ask me that, Megan?"

"The day Paul was killed, Kelly was in the store and

mentioned that Paul wouldn't let her hire The Wright Men For The Job anymore. He told her he didn't trust you."

He stops working and pops his head out from inside the dishwasher.

"If anyone isn't trustworthy, it's Paul."

He places the tool he was using back in the toolbox and pulls out a different tool.

"Six weeks ago or so, Paul offered to pay me to burglarize Hairway To Heaven."

He pauses and waits for me to respond. I'm taken aback and need a few seconds to catch up.

"Why would he want to steal from his wife's business? What did he want you to steal? Shampoo and conditioner?" I ask, spinning my ring.

"Kelly's been investing in new equipment this year, including two new computers, new styling tools, and other stuff that Paul said isn't cheap. His plan was to keep Kelly away from the salon and apartment for a night and give me a list of what to take. I'd steal the items on the list and deliver them to a buyer he had lined up, collect the cash from the buyer, give half the cash to Paul and keep the other half for my trouble. He told me it wasn't really stealing because everything is insured, so she'd be able to file an insurance claim and replace it all."

Theft and insurance fraud. That's a big deal, and a big thing to ask your local handyman to help you out with.

"What did you tell him when he asked you to do it?"

Ryan chuckles.

"I told him no way. But he didn't like that answer, and told me if I didn't do it, he'd tell everyone I'm a felon."

I close the door to the kitchenette because in Harmony Lake, all the walls have ears.

"Are you a felon, Ryan?" I ask, barely above a whisper.

"Technically, yes," he replies matter-of-factly. "Remember about five years ago when I moved to Ottawa to work for my Uncle's construction company?"

I nod.

"Well, I wasn't in a very good place back then, and I made some bad decisions. I found out some guys on the site were stealing copper wire, among other things, and reselling them. They offered to cut me in if I didn't say anything, and I accepted. For the next few months, they kept stealing from worksites, and I kept pretending not to notice. Once a week one of the guys would buy me a coffee from the coffee truck, but it was an empty cup filled with cash. What I didn't know was that one of them was an undercover cop who infiltrated the group to bring down the theft ring. I was charged along with everyone else. I copped a plea and spent three months in jail."

"Wow, Ryan. I had no idea. How did Paul know? Did you tell him?"

"After I was released, I was on probation. Every other week for three years, I would drive into the city to visit my probation officer. Paul saw me go into the probation office a couple of times and snooped around. He was probably in the city visiting the casino."

Ryan ducks back into the dishwasher and continues working.

Paul seems to have a habit of blackmailing people, first Adam, and now Ryan. Maybe that's what he and Fred were arguing about in the car. Maybe Paul was blackmailing the Murphys, too. But how would he have known that Stephanie Murphy was the woman Adam was seeing? Could he have seen them together in the city, like he saw Ryan in the city visiting his probation officer?

"So how did you avoid being blackmailed? I mean, he didn't tell anyone, right?"

He pops out of the dishwasher.

"Paul likes to gamble. It used to be a big problem for him, but he learned to control it after Kelly threatened to leave him if he didn't stop. Lately, he hasn't been able to keep it under control, and he's had to borrow money to hide his gambling debt from Kelly. I told him I know about his gambling habit and debt and that I'd tell Kelly about it and about his plan to rob the salon. He hasn't talked to me since, and it sounds like he lied to Kelly to make sure she wouldn't talk to me either."

"How do you know about Paul's gambling debt?"

"I do a lot of work for Jay Singh. He's a money lender who lives in Harmony Hills. We've become friends. He's super smart, so when Paul tried to blackmail me, I asked Jay for advice. Jay told me that he loaned Paul money to pay off his gambling debt, and Paul was having trouble making the repayments. He told me to use that information to get away from Paul, and he also hoped it would put some pressure on Paul to get his payments up to date. And before you ask, I happened to be with Jay when Paul was murdered. He hired me to assemble one of those backyard play sets for his twins."

Ryan's head and shoulders disappear into the

dishwasher, and I open the door to the kitchenette and return to the store.

Ryan finishes replacing the thingamajig and puts the dishwasher back together. He gives Connie an invoice, she pays him out of the till, and he leaves.

WHEN WE'RE ALONE, I disclose to Connie what Ryan told me. I know I can trust her to keep Ryan's past to herself. She doesn't seem as shocked as I thought she'd be about Ryan's criminal past, but she is just as shocked as I was about Paul's scheme to burgle the salon.

This means there are other people, whose last name isn't Martel, with a motive to kill Paul.

If Hairway To Heaven had been robbed, I'm pretty sure the whole town would know, so I assume Paul wasn't able to pull it off. Maybe he tried to hire someone else to rob the salon, it didn't work out, and they killed him. Or maybe the buyer he lined up for the equipment killed him when the equipment wasn't delivered.

If he owes money to Jay Singh, perhaps Jay Singh killed him. That wouldn't be good for business though, since dead men don't make debt repayments. But sometimes on TV, the loan shark kills the person who owes them money as a warning to the other people who owe them money.

Maybe Kelly found out about the robbery plot, the gambling, the debt, or all of the above, and it pushed her over the edge, and she killed him.

Maybe he was using the photos of Adam and Stephanie to blackmail the Murphys, and they killed him.

Or, maybe Ryan is lying. If he is lying, it's an elaborate lie. There's only one way to find out for sure.

"Since I'm not scheduled to work this afternoon, I'm going to visit Jay Singh."

"That doesn't sound very safe, my dear. What if he is the killer?"

"I promise I'll only go if April comes with me."

I make an X over my heart with my right hand to assure Connie that I mean it.

"We won't go inside anywhere alone with him. At the very least, he might verify Ryan's alibi and remove him from the list of suspects."

Connie doesn't say anything. Instead, she purses her lips and squints slightly. The look on her face makes it clear that she doesn't like my plan but won't try to stop me.

"I have a book club meeting tonight, and Archie is a member, so I'll ask him if he remembers where Ryan was when Paul was murdered."

"Thank you," I say, and smile at her.

I pull out my phone and text April, asking her if she's up for a road trip this afternoon. She is! We agree to meet after lunch and drive to Harmony Hills.

I get another text from Eric asking when we can meet. I decide to holdback my reply until after April and I visit Jay. Hopefully, then, I'll be able to give him a lead on a suspect that isn't Adam or me.

CHAPTER 12

I LEAVE Knitorious and drop off the online orders at the post office on my way home for a quick lunch before April and I go to Jay Singh's house. It's still cloudy and humid, but the drizzle has stopped for now. I feel my curly hair expanding in the damp air and use the hair elastic on my wrist to pull it into a high ponytail while I walk.

Walking up to the house, it's weird to see Adam's car in the driveway in the middle of a weekday. Walking into the house, it's even weirder to see him sitting at the kitchen table in the middle of a weekday. He's working intently on his new laptop, and I don't want to disturb him, so I walk into the kitchen without saying anything.

"Hey!" He says without looking up.

"Hey. How's the new laptop?"

"I like it. I had to leave my old laptop with the firm when I resigned, it's company property. Anyway, I need a laptop if I'm going to start my own practice in Harmony Lake."

He looks at me and smiles.

"Oh, you aren't looking to join another firm?"

I assumed he'd pursue a partnership elsewhere.

"No, it's time for a change," he replies. "I can't work anywhere for thirty days because of the thirty day non-compete clause I have with the firm, but on the thirty-first day, I intend to hang out my shingle and open for business. There aren't any lawyers in Harmony Lake right now, so it's an underserved market. The closest lawyer is at least half an hour away in Harmony Hills, and I think his practice is limited to real estate law, if he's still there. He might be retired now. I should look into that, actually."

He picks up a pen and makes a note in the planner beside his laptop.

"How was your visit to the police station last night? I didn't hear you come in, so you must've been there pretty late"

He makes a sweeping gesture with his hand, "It was fine. I answered all of Eric's questions as honestly and as thoroughly as I could. He asked to keep my cell phone though, so I went out this morning and bought this."

He holds up a shiny new cell phone in one hand and waves the other hand under it with a flourish that would make Vanna White proud.

"It's two models newer than the one Eric kept. It's really advanced, and it can interact with Oscar!"

Getting new technology is Adam's happy place.

"I already texted Hannah, so she has my new number."

"How did you explain that to her?"

She knows Paul was murdered, but I'm trying to avoid telling her that her parents are murder suspects.

"Relax," he says, "I told her I left the firm to open my own practice in Harmony Lake and the laptop and the phone both belong to the firm, and I had to leave them there when I resigned. She's fine with it."

He taps on the screen of his new phone then puts it down on the table.

My phone dings; a text from a number I don't recognize.

"I assume this is from you?" I ask.

"Yup, now you have my new number," he nods.

I save his number to my phone and delete his old office and cell phone numbers.

"Adam."

"Mm hmm." He's staring at his laptop screen again.

"Adam. Look at me."

We make eye contact.

"Are you having an affair with Kelly Sinclair?"

His eyes open as wide as they can, and his eyebrows raise up as high as they can go without disappearing into his hairline.

"Of course not, Meg! Why would you even ask me that?"

"Then why have you been communicating with her and meeting her?"

"Did Kelly mention this to you?" He looks confused.

"No, Eric did. He asked me if I knew why you and Kelly were communicating and if I knew about you meeting with her. I told him I don't know anything, because I don't."

He's hesitant to respond, and I can tell he's choosing his words carefully.

"It would be inappropriate for me to comment on any communication between myself and Kelly Sinclair."

His lawyer voice. I'm no longer speaking to Adam my soon-to-be-ex-husband but to Adam the lawyer. I know this routine well.

"Is your relationship with Kelly protected by attorney-client privilege?" I ask.

He puts his right hand in front of his chest palm toward the floor and turns his wrist. "It's complicated."

"Complicated because you have a personal, intimate relationship with her?"

C'mon Adam, give me a clue.

"No! Absolutely not! Stephanie is the only personal relationship I've had, and it was a huge mistake on so many levels. I've regretted it every day since it started. This summer, by the way. Long after you and I called it quits."

Not that long, but whatever.

"Kelly's not a client. She hasn't paid me for legal services, and I haven't represented her. Technically, we spoke as friends. I didn't even let her pay for my coffee, so I'm not violating attorney-client privilege if I tell you."

I take the seat across from him at the kitchen table, and he closes his laptop.

"Kelly texted me a couple of months ago and wanted to meet for coffee, but not here, in Harmony Lake, and not near my office. We met at a coffee shop in the city where she told me that once upon a time, Paul had a gambling problem and racked up significant debt. The gambling and the financial strain almost ended their marriage, but he got help for his gambling, they decided to stay together, and over time they paid off the debt. Now that they're back on their financial feet and the business is doing well, Kelly was worried about what could happen if Paul gambled again. About her potential liability for any gambling debts he might incur. She wanted advice on Paul-proofing the business and the building. We talked about various hypothetical options and scenarios for about an hour. After that, she never contacted me again, but Paul did. A few days after Kelly and I met, Paul began texting me, demanding to know why I met with Kelly. He accused me of having an affair with her or trying to."

"What did you tell him? And did you let Kelly know that Paul was contacting you?"

"I denied it." He shrugs. "I pretended I had no idea what he was talking about. When he kept texting after that, I ignored his texts. He phoned and left a couple of voicemail messages, but I never returned his calls. I saved the messages, they're on the phone the police kept. In one of the messages, he said he knows Kelly and I have been talking because he saw the text messages when he went through her phone, and he knows we met because he saw the entry in the calendar on her phone. I never told Kelly about it. She wasn't my client, and I didn't want to have any more involvement with Paul than I already had."

"Wow. It's starting to sound like Paul wasn't just bossy

and controlling in his role as a town councilor, but in his role as husband, too." I get up to get a glass of water and process what Adam just told me.

"Meg, I didn't kill Paul."

"I know."

"Have you given a statement yet?"

I'm not sure if Adam the lawyer is asking or Adam the soon-to-be-ex-husband.

"Kind of, I guess. I answered questions that night, again yesterday morning at the store, and yesterday evening when Eric came to see you. He's been texting me and asking if we can meet today, so he can ask me more questions. Surely, he's running out of things to ask me by now."

"You should have a lawyer present when he questions you. Let me give you a number..." He opens his laptop and starts tapping on the keyboard.

"I don't need a lawyer, Adam, it's fine. I haven't done anything wrong and I have nothing to hide. I'd rather tell him everything I know and do whatever I can to help find the killer, so I can stop suspecting everyone I know of being a murderer, and we can get on with our lives."

Did Paul make a habit of spying on Kelly? Why didn't he trust her? If she knew he was violating her privacy and checking up on her, would that make her angry enough to kill him?

Based on the conversation she had with Adam, it sounds like she knew, or at least suspected, that Paul was gambling again.

CHAPTER 13

THANKS TO LIVING in the age of technology, a quick web search helped me find Jay Singh's address in Harmony Hills and the GPS in April's car is helping us get there. It's raining, and we're on the highway almost halfway between Harmony Lake and Harmony Hills. Harmony Lake is on the south side of the Harmony Hills Mountains, nestled snugly between the mountains and the lake. Harmony Hills is located on the north side of the Harmony Hills Mountains and is a suburb of the city located farther north. Harmony Hills is larger than Harmony Lake and doesn't have the same geographic restrictions, so it has a larger population and more amenities. Most residents of Harmony Lake find themselves making regular trips to Harmony Hills to visit the hospital, big box stores, various professionals, movie theatres, and everything else Harmony Hills has that our tiny town doesn't. The quickest route to get from

Harmony Lake to Harmony hills is a twenty to thirty-minute drive along the highway just outside town that runs past, or technically through the mountains.

April and I agree that it feels pushy showing up at a stranger's home unannounced, but I'm hoping the element of surprise will work to our advantage; he might not agree to speak to us if he has time to think about it, and his reactions will be more candid than they would be if he had time to prepare for our visit.

THE SINGH HOME IS A TWO-STOREY, two-car garage, detached, red-brick house, located in a newer subdivision with several speed bumps and no shortage of DRIVE SLOWLY: CHILDREN AT PLAY signs posted above the many NEIGHBOURHOOD WATCH signs. The front lawn and garden are meticulously maintained, and the top of the driveway is littered with two tiny, training-wheeled bikes, hula hoops, a small basketball net, and remnants of chalk drawings that have been almost completely washed away by the rain.

We pull up outside the house. It's not raining right now, but everything is wet. A thirtyish year-old man wearing cargo shorts, a t-shirt and rain boots is jumping in puddles on the sidewalk with two small children. Both are wearing identical bright green raincoats with frog eyes on the hoods and yellow rubber boots with toes painted like duck bills and eyes on the tops of the feet. They're freakin' adorable!

"Ryan mentioned that Jay has twins, so that's probably him," I say to April whose eyes are also fixed on the two identical, adorable puddle jumpers.

"Aww, look at them!" she says. "We should go and talk to him before our ovaries explode, or the neighbourhood watch starts to wonder why we're sitting here."

We unbuckle our seat belts and April unplugs her phone from the car's console. We get out of the car and the sound of the horn confirming that the doors are locked gets the attention of the boys, so I smile and wave at them. They ignore me and jump in a puddle.

I introduce myself to Jay as a friend of Ryan's, and April introduces herself as a friend of mine. We shake hands and April and I gush over the cuteness of his sons. I tell him he has two of the cutest frog-duck puddle jumpers I've ever seen, and he smiles at them proudly.

"If you're looking for a loan, there are online forms to fill out on the website, and I'll get back to you within twenty-four hours."

He must be a modern, twenty-first century money lender.

"No. I'm not here for a loan, but since you brought it up, I am super curious about your business, is it a legitimate business? You have a website and everything?"

"Of course. Everything is totally above board. The service I provide is more common than you think."

He proceeds to tell us he's a stay-at-home dad, and his sons just turned four. He and his wife, Jenna, were both nurses at Harmony Hills hospital, but after the twins arrived, finding an affordable daycare situation to accommodate their erratic shift schedules was nearly impossible, so they decided Jay would stay home.

They had some money from an inheritance, and to replace Jay's income they were going to purchase one of the luxury condos in the new Harbourview Condominium development at the end of Water Street and rent it to tourists. Unfortunately the development was still almost a year away from starting construction, and they couldn't wait that long. Jay did some research and realized that the return on investment would be higher and the risk more diversified if they used the money to make several high interest, short term loans, so they did that instead.

I can relate to their daycare struggle. I found out I was expecting Hannah within a few months of getting married, and about five years sooner than we'd planned for it to happen, so I had to leave school when she arrived, three semesters short of my economics degree. When she started school full time, I was eager to finish my last three semesters and graduate, but I couldn't find a daycare solution that worked for all three of us. I was about to give up and accept that I'd have to wait to finish school, when Connie insisted that she and Colin, her husband, would love to help look after Hannah. They were like grandparents to her and spoiled her rotten. Sadly, Colin passed away about five years ago, but Connie and Hannah still have a special bond.

"What I do is totally legal, though some people might think it isn't totally ethical. Most of my clients are in Harmony Hills and Harmony Lake, and my job makes me privy to a lot of secrets about a lot of people."

He winks after that last sentence, and I get the feeling he'd love to tell some of those secrets, but I already feel like I'm learning more about some of my neighbours than I care to know, so I decide to interrupt him.

"That's actually why I'm here. I'd like to ask you some questions about a mutual acquaintance. Ryan tells me you know Paul Sinclair?"

"What about him? Does he owe you money?" He smirks.

Hearing him talk about Paul in the present tense makes me think he doesn't know about Paul's death, so I tell him Paul was murdered on Tuesday evening.

"Well, that's too bad. I guess I should expect a visit from the police soon," He says bluntly.

He seems neither surprised by Paul's death nor worried about a visit from the police.

"Ryan told me that when Paul was trying to blackmail him, you helped him out by giving him some information to use against Paul. Well, unfortunately, when Paul was killed, he was also blackmailing my family, and I'm looking for information that might point the finger of suspicion away from us."

"He borrowed money from me. I think he said it was to pay off some bad bets. He had trouble paying me back and fell behind with his scheduled repayments. He stopped returning my calls and emails, so my lawyer wrote a letter to Mr. and Mrs. Sinclair advising them that I was starting the process of executing a writ of seizure on the building on Water Street."

I know about writs of seizure from Adam mentioning

them. A writ of seizure would give Jay the right to force the Sinclairs to sell the building and use the proceeds to repay the debt.

"But the business belongs to Kelly, not Paul," April interrupts. "Did they borrow money from you together?"

"No, Paul borrowed the money alone. One of the reasons people borrow from me, instead of a bank, and pay higher interest costs, is because they don't want their partner to know about the loan. His wife might own the business in her name alone, but they both own the building, so they both have to be notified. The letter and the threat are usually enough to scare the debtor into finding my money."

"Was it enough to scare Paul?" I ask.

"Sure was. I heard from him the day he got the letter. It was sent by registered mail, and he's the one who signed for it, so I doubt his wife ever saw it. A few days later he asked to meet and paid the loan in full. With cash."

"Where did he get that much cash in such a short time?"

I'm looking at April and thinking out loud, not expecting Jay to say anything, but he does.

"He said his brother-in-law lent it to him. I don't know if that's true, and I don't really care. People who need my services tend to have secrets and often lie to protect them, so I take most of what they say with a grain of salt."

One of the twins asks if they can go in the backyard to dig for worms. Both boys are carrying a small bucket and shovel. So cute!

We walk from the sidewalk to the gate at the side of the house. April hangs back close to the sidewalk. I know she's being safe so if something happens, she can get help. Jay opens the gate and the boys run into the backyard. There's a large wooden play set with a slide on one side, two swings in the middle, and a playhouse with a rock-climbing wall on the other side.

"That must be the playset Ryan assembled on Tuesday?" I ask, pointing to the large wooden structure.

"He assembled it, but, like, two weeks ago, not on Tuesday," Jay replies.

As soon as the words finish coming out of his mouth, the expression on his face changes and I can tell Jay realizes that he probably just contradicted Ryan's alibi

"Actually, I can't remember for sure. Maybe Ryan was here on Tuesday night?"

He furrows his brow, purses his lips, and directs his gaze down and to the right, trying hard to look like he's working out the correct date.

Nice try, Jay.

"Look, Ryan's a good guy," he asserts. "He's made a few mistakes and bad choices, but I consider him a friend. He must consider you a friend, too, if he told you about me and sent you here. There's no way he killed Paul."

We hear one twin offer up his dessert tonight in exchange for the other twin eating a worm. But it has to be the whole worm, not just a bite.

Jay runs over to stop anyone from eating any portion of any worm. I yell after him, thanking him for his time, wishing him good luck with the worms, and telling him April and I will see ourselves out.

He waves to me in acknowledgement.

CHAPTER 14

"WELL, that was definitely worth the drive," I say as April navigates the car out of Jay's subdivision.

"I know, right?! He said he has clients in Harmony Hills and is 'privy to lots of secrets.' I wonder who else in Harmony Hills borrows money from him?"

"I'm not sure I want to know," I answer. "Life was easier forty-eight hours ago when the only secrets I knew were my own."

"And mine, you know all my secrets," April adds.

"How can we find Paul's brother-in-law to ask him if he loaned Paul the money? And if Ryan lied about being at Jay's house on Tuesday evening, where was he and why would he lie?"

"I don't know the answer to either of those questions," April says as she turns onto the main road that leads to the highway, "but I do know that solving a murder in real life is harder than it looks on TV and in books."

She's not wrong.

My phone dings; another text from Eric trying to arrange a time and place to meet. I don't fancy being questioned at the police station. I assume Adam will be home tonight, and I don't want to make him go out. Luckily, Connie has a book club meeting and since it isn't her turn to host, Knitorious will be empty.

I text him back and suggest we meet at Knitorious after it closes. He confirms.

April puts on No Scrubs by TLC and turns it up loud. We sing about a scrub *hanging out the passenger side of his best friends ride* at the top of our lungs as we merge onto the highway.

I GET to Knitorious about twenty minutes before the store closes, park in one of the spots behind the store and let myself in through the back door.

Harlow is happy to see me because my arrival coincides with his dinnertime. He corners me in the kitchenette and charms me into feeding him.

Connie is relieved I'm still alive, and the money lender didn't kill April and me.

I fill her in on our trip to Harmony Hills and remind her to please ask Archie about Ryan's whereabouts on Tuesday night since Jay didn't confirm his alibi.

"He told you himself that he's not ethical, my dear. Maybe Ryan was there, and the money lender is mistaken or lying. But, of course, I'll ask. If I can get him alone."

"He told me that some people believe his business is unethical, not that he's unethical. Also, you didn't see his reaction when he realized what he'd said."

I offer to close up so she can leave early and meet her book club friends. I tell her that Eric is coming to the store with more questions for me, but we should be gone before she gets home.

I didn't have dinner before coming to the store, so by the time Eric is due to arrive I'm starving and scrolling through the menu on the Ho Lee Chow website, adding items to the online cart. I stop scrolling to unlock the door for Eric when he arrives. I don't recognize him at first because he's not wearing a suit.

He's wearing khaki, slim-fit trousers and a dark green, collared Polo shirt with brown leather slip-on shoes. The dark green shirt brings out the amber flecks in his eyes and the short sleeves show off a pair of nicely defined, muscular biceps and forearms. He's hot, and I have to remind myself not to stare.

"Hi! Thanks for meeting me again," he says, standing aside, so I can lock the door after him.

He smells good, like a forest after it rains, and the sun comes out.

"No problem. You must be running out of questions by now, no? Or will I be answering the same questions I've already answered?"

I wonder if he's met with everyone else three times in two days, or just the top contenders on his suspect list.

"A bit of both." He smiles and puts a hand on his flat, probably-has-a-six-pack stomach.

Don't stare, Megan.

"Have you eaten? I'm starving and I thought I might order something to be delivered if that's OK."

"Great minds think alike, Eric." I spin the laptop to show him the Ho Lee Chow menu I've been picking and choosing from.

He adds a few items to our order, and I hit the Submit button. While we wait for the food to arrive, I get dishes from the kitchenette, Harlow forces Eric to notice him by jumping onto the harvest table and pacing back and forth in front of him with his tail in the air, and Eric asks me questions about yarn.

What's the difference between a hank, a skein, a ball, and a cake? I explain that a hank is a loop of yarn that's loosely twisted, similar to the yarn that Kelly bought. A skein is yarn that's wound into an oblong ball. A ball is yarn that's wound into a round ball, and a cake is yarn that's wound into a cylindrical shape. To confuse him further, I explain how the words "hank" and "skein" are often used interchangeably. I gather yarn from the shelves as I explain to show him examples of each.

What does ply mean? Well, yarn is composed of multiple yarns twisted together: single ply is one strand of yarn, two-ply is two strands twisted together, three-ply is three strands twisted together, etc. The yarn Kelly purchased was twelve-ply.

He also has questions about knitting needles: straight vs. circular, metal vs. wood, how to decide which size needle to use with which size yarn. At first, I assume his curiosity is related to the case, but then I start to wonder if he's actually interested and wants to learn to knit. I'm sure it's related to the case, but I offer to teach him to knit anyway. He declines. Apparently, his job keeps him too busy for hobbies like knitting.

When he's finished testing my yarn and needle knowledge, we sit in the cozy sitting area and I pick up the hat I'm working on. I start the crown decreases while he asks me questions about my routine on Tuesday, and strokes Harlow, who is curled up contentedly on his lap.

Our food arrives, and while we eat, he asks me about yesterday. I tell him, again, about Adam visiting me at the store and telling me that Paul had copies of the photos and was using them to blackmail him. Then I tell him how caught off guard I was last night by the suggestion that Adam and Kelly were having an affair.

"I'm sorry about the way that played out, and that you were upset," he says. "I didn't think there was anything between them, but I needed to be sure, and your reaction helped confirm my hunch."

I appreciate his apology, but I don't respond because I still think it was a cruel way to confirm his hunch.

"Finding out about the affair with Mrs. Murphy must have upset you though…"

Eric likes to use unfinished sentences to ask questions. He makes a statement and lets his voice trail off at the end while he looks at you to finish the thought for him.

"Adam and I have been married for almost 20 years. We met in university when I was 18, and by the time I was

20, we were married, and I became pregnant soon after. We had a great relationship for a lot of years, but somewhere along the way we started to grow apart. Our lives stopped revolving around each other and neither of us did anything to stop it. He focused on his career, I focused on being a Mom and being involved in the community, and the next thing we knew our daughter was the only thing we had left in common."

I stop to drink some water.

"If you both decided it was over months ago, why are you still living under the same roof and keeping your separation a secret? The divorced couples I know can't wait to get away from each other."

I want to ask him if he's speaking from experience, but I don't.

"This year has been a big one for Hannah. She finished high school and went away to university. We were determined not to allow our separation to overshadow her final year of high school, so we decided he wouldn't move out until she left for university. The last thing she needed was everyone in town talking about our failed marriage and her broken home. Reputation is everything in a small town—especially in Harmony Lake. We're handling this transition like civilized, reasonable people. I've always put Hannah's interests above all else, and this divorce is no exception. We may not be a couple anymore, but we're Hannah's parents and we'll always be family. It helps that Adam is a lawyer. He works on divorce cases all the time and sees how divorce can bring out the worst in people. That won't happen to us. We're intent on making it through this divorce and coming out the other side as friends. Or at least friendly to each other. We'll see."

"No one else in Harmony Lake knows you're separated?" Eric asks.

"The only people who know, other than Hannah, are April and Connie, unless Adam confided in someone. I don't feel angry or betrayed that he was seeing someone. I mean, I haven't been in love with him for a long time, you know? I want him to be happy and live a good life. I just wish he'd waited until he moved out, didn't send his girlfriend compromising photos, and maybe picked someone who isn't already in a relationship."

It feels cathartic to say it out loud for someone else to hear. It's not easy pretending your marriage isn't broken. Living a lie is exhausting.

I wonder if Eric is married and has kids. Has he ever had to disentangle his life from someone else's while causing as little damage as possible to the other people affected?

It's like playing catch with a hand grenade, except every time you throw it, you have to take one step backwards until eventually you and the person you're playing catch with can't communicate anymore. So, you both just try to be slow, gentle, and intentional with every toss, grateful every time the other person catches it, and it doesn't hit the ground and blow up destroying your home, everyone else's lives, and your kid.

When we've finished eating, we each choose a fortune cookie. Eric's says, "You are cleverly disguised as a responsible adult," and mine says, "Three people can keep a secret only if you get rid of two," which sounds ominous and creeps me out. I jokingly offer to trade fortunes with him, but he declines, saying he likes his non-creepy fortune better.

While I clear the dishes and throw away the food packages, I contemplate whether to tell him about my conversation this morning with Ryan and the road trip April and I took to Harmony Hills to visit Jay this afternoon. I want this case solved as quickly as possible, and the more information Eric has, the quicker he can find the real killer and clear the Martel name, so I decide it's best to tell him.

If I'm lucky, maybe he'll tell me something in return that I don't already know about the case.

"I had an interesting conversation with Ryan Wright this morning."

While I tell him about my conversation with Ryan, I watch his face closely for a hint of a reaction. Nothing. Either he already knows and this isn't new information, or he's got an impressive poker face.

I double down and tell him about my conversation with Jay. Still no reaction.

When I finish talking, he gazes into the distance like he's thinking about something. Then he looks at me.

"I'm not from Harmony Lake," he states. "This is a small community and the residents are...protective...of each other and of information. They don't trust outsiders, and I'm an outsider, so they're hesitant to open up to me."

He's choosing his words carefully. I'm a resident of this

small, protective community, and he doesn't want to offend me, a nice change from last night.

He's right, it takes a long time for us to warm up to new people and accept them as one of us. We cater to tourists who are only here for a few days or weeks of the year. Some of them want the local experience while they're here, and we've learned to make them feel welcome and included while still protecting the heart of our community and keeping it just for us.

"I appreciate you sharing what you've found out with me," he says, "but it's not a good idea for you to investigate on your own and question witnesses. Asking the wrong questions to the wrong people could put your safety at risk. But if people seek you out and share information with you, I'd really appreciate you passing that information along to me."

I'm choosing to interpret this as a verbal disclaimer, like an 'Enter At Your Own Risk' sign at a construction site. It doesn't mean you *can't* enter the site; it just means if you do, you might get hurt, and it'll be your own fault because you ignored the sign warning you it's risky. Am I interpreting him incorrectly? Maybe, but he didn't say no, he said it's not a good idea, and that isn't the same as no.

While it would be easier and less work for both of us if he would just say what he means, I'm learning that Eric speaks in subtext. He answers questions without actually answering them, and now it seems he gives permission without actually giving permission. It must be a cop thing.

It's getting late and it's been a long day. I try to fight it, but a yawn escapes me, and I ask Eric if we're done with questions for the night. I turn off the lights, we both say goodnight to Harlow, and he follows us to the back door and then slinks up the stairs to Connie's apartment. Eric and I leave through the back door. We wish each other a good weekend, which makes me hopeful that he's not planning to question me again until at least Monday.

CHAPTER 15

FRIDAY, September 13th

I'm on my own at the store because Connie has yet another mystery appointment this morning. She's had a few appointments lately, but doesn't tell me where she's going, only when she's going, which is unusual for her. I hope everything is OK and have to trust her to tell me if it isn't.

Friday and Saturday are our busiest days, so business is steady today. Harlow, planting his cuteness in a warm ray of sun in the front window for his morning nap, attracts a few passersby who come into the store to see him, making us appear even busier.

Paul's murder is still the number one conversation topic for people who stop to chat, and people are starting to ask when the crime scene tape will be removed from Hairway To Heaven.

I take advantage of the short intervals between serving

customers to update the inventory on the website and finish Hannah's hat; I bind it off just before noon.

When Connie returns from her appointment, she brings me a sandwich from Deliclassy. It must be tuna because Harlow is up on the counter in a flash, seriously interested in the bag.

"How was book club? It was pretty late when I left, but you still weren't back."

"It was fun! There was some confusion about what our September book is, so half of us showed up having read one book and half of us read another book. We solved it by breaking into two smaller groups, one for each book, and next month we'll switch!"

"I'm glad it worked out. Did you happen to get a chance to ask Archie about Ryan's whereabouts on Tuesday evening?"

"Yes, I did. Archie insists Ryan was with him. They watched the baseball game on TV and barbecued steaks. He says Ryan was with him from late afternoon until the next morning."

"I guess Ryan mixed up his Tuesdays, then. He must have been in Harmony Hills the previous Tuesday," I shrug.

"I've known Archie a long time, my dear. He wouldn't lie. I believe him."

"So do I," I say.

At least I think I do. I want to. Would Archie lie to give his son an alibi? I think a lot of parents would be surprised at the lengths they'd go to protect their children.

Harlow and I eat my sandwich in the kitchenette, and the rest of the afternoon passes quickly.

We close the store and tidy up in preparation for tomorrow. Then I go home to have an awkward dinner with Adam. Since our meals together usually include Hannah, I can't remember the last time we had a meal where it was just the two of us. We struggle to find something to talk about that isn't either Paul's murder, or Hannah.

As much as I enjoy a good small town murder mystery or true crime documentary, both feel a bit too close to home right now. After dinner, I watch a stand-up comedy special, cast on the matching cowl for Hannah's hat, and knit until my eyelids feel heavy and I'm ready for bed.

SATURDAY, September 14th

Connie and I both work on Saturdays because it's the busiest day of the week, and today is no exception. We're getting into our busy season. Knitters are starting to embrace fall and plan ahead for holiday knitting. As soon as the snow starts to fall, we'll also be busy with tourists staying at the ski resorts in Harmony Hills. Saturdays are only going to get busier from now until after ski season.

After lunch, Connie's phone chimes. She reads the message then hands me her phone, so I can read it. There are customers milling around the store, and she doesn't want to read it out loud.

It's a message in the WSBA group chat:

Lizzie: Paul's body has been released to his family. His funeral is scheduled for Wednesday. It will be a private service for family only followed by a public celebration of life at The Irish Embassy. More details to come.

Lizzie is the owner of Latte Da, and The Irish Embassy is our local pub. The Embassy, as it's called by the locals, is owned by the O'Brien family. Sheamus manages the pub, and his parents, who are mostly retired, divide their time between Harmony Lake and Dublin, Ireland.

I hand Connie's phone back to her, and literally seconds later, a symphony of cell phone notifications can be heard throughout the store. Customers begin talking about the news that Paul's body has been released and his funeral arrangements are being made. It's incredible how fast news travels though Harmony Lake.

Tonight is trivia night at The Embassy. The knitting group that meets at the store each week has formed a team called Knitty By Nature. The winning team gets a free meal (lunch only) at the pub. Tamara meets us at the store after it closes and we head over to The Embassy to win that free lunch! Tamara is a trivia buff and an occasional knitter, so we recruited her for our team. She's alone tonight because April is taking their fifteen-year-old son, Zach, to hockey practice. We don't win the free lunch, but thanks to Tamara, we come in a close second.

Everyone in the pub is speculating about Paul's murder, and asking Sheamus for details about Paul's funeral arrangements, but Sheamus isn't talking. He doesn't confirm or deny anything, and says he'll tell us more when details are confirmed.

SUNDAY, September 15th

This is the third Sunday since Hannah's left home, and so far, Sundays are when I miss her the most. It's the one day when we were usually both home and would do something fun together. On Sunday evenings we would have dinner as a family when Adam came home.

Since we can't be together as a family in person, we do the next best thing. Adam and I FaceTime Hannah together and have a virtual visit with her. She tells us about her classes, her new friends, and the fun, touristy things she's doing in Toronto.

We're careful not to mention Paul's murder, blackmail schemes, or being questioned by the police. When Hannah mentions Paul, she asks how Kelly is doing, and I tell her that Kelly has been staying with her sister in Harmony Hills, then Adam and I quickly change the subject.

Several times each day, I have the urge to text Kelly to see how she is and let her know everyone is thinking about her, but I don't want to impose. She has so much going on, and as far as I know, she hasn't been back to Harmony Lake since Paul died. If she's not ready to deal with us yet, I don't want to force us on her.

I spend the rest of Sunday missing Hannah, cleaning the house around Adam while he works on his laptop, and giving the lawn and garden some much-needed maintenance.

CHAPTER 16

MONDAY, September 16th

Knitorious is closed on Mondays, so that's when I usually drive to Harmony Hills to grocery shop and run whatever other errands I can't do in Harmony Lake.

I pull into a parking spot in the Shop'n'Save parking lot, turn the car off, pull out my phone, and send a text to April:

Me: I'm in HH today, do you need anything?

Whenever one of us comes to Harmony Hills, we text the other to see if they need anything while we're here. It's become a habit.

I push the button that opens the trunk and get out of the car to retrieve my reusable shopping bags. I close the trunk and feel my phone vibrate in my pocket.

April: So am I! I was about to text you. I just got to Shop'n'Save. About to go in.

Me: I'm in the parking lot, where are you?

April: Meet me at the door by the pharmacy.

I put my phone back in my pocket and head toward the pharmacy entrance where I find and hug my friend.

"Why are you here on a Monday? You know I shop on Mondays. I would've picked up whatever you need," I say.

"I know, it's weird to be here on a Monday, but we have this...situation...called Zach. He's fifteen and eats CONSTANTLY, so I'm having to shop three times a week just to keep him fed. Also, they're having a ridiculous sale on butter this week, and T wants me to buy as many bricks as I can carry. She's afraid they'll run out before the sale ends."

"If there's a limit on how many you can buy, I'll buy up to the limit, too, so T won't have butter anxiety," I offer.

We each get a cart and decide to start in the butter section, just in case.

April puts the maximum amount of butter each shopper is allowed to purchase at the sale price into her cart and so do I.

Our carts stacked with literally enough butter to supply a bakery, we meander up and down the aisles, picking up items and checking them off our lists as we go. We talk about our weekends, update each other on Hannah and Rachel, and strategize to get Tamara on Jeopardy, so she can win all the money, and she and April can retire.

We turn into the freezer aisle and April is telling me she doesn't think Tamara would retire even if she won on Jeopardy because she loves working at the bakery too much to give it up, when I'm sure I see Kelly Sinclair walk past the end of the aisle pushing a cart, accompanied by a woman I don't recognize.

I tighten my grip on the handle of my butter-heavy cart and speed walk to the end of the aisle trying to catch up to her. April speed walks after me.

"Where are we going? I need to get frozen pizza in this aisle."

"I'm sure I just saw Kelly walk by," I say.

I make a sharp left, speed walk past a display of peanut butter, then toilet paper, and look up the next aisle. No Kelly. I keep going toward the next aisle, past a display of tomato sauce, then baby food. April breaks into a jog, and in a few strides, she and her butter-filled cart are walking beside me.

"Kelly Sinclair?" she asks.

"Yes. With a woman. They have a cart."

I look up the next aisle, no Kelly. April uses her impossibly long legs to outpace me and gets to the next aisle. She looks up the aisle, then looks back at me.

"Found them!"

She smiles and turns her cart into the household cleaning aisle. My cart and I follow her up the aisle, and I think about how this would never happen in Harmony Lake; the stores are too small for a foot chase. There are clearly benefits to small stores with short aisles.

Kelly is at the other end of the aisle. Her hair is pulled into a messy bun, and she's wearing grey sweatpants, a matching grey sweatshirt, and white running shoes. She looks so different from the polished, glamourous Kelly I'm used to seeing in Harmony Lake that I'm surprised I recognized her. She's facing a shelf, and seems to be comparing two items, with one in each hand.

Her friend and I make eye contact. I don't recognize her. She's definitely not from Harmony Lake. She says something to Kelly, then turns and walks away from her, disappearing as she turns at the end of the aisle.

When we're about halfway up the aisle where Kelly is comparing what appears to be disinfectant wipes, April calls her name.

Kelly turns toward us and her face lights up with recognition. April pulls her cart over to the side of the aisle, walks over to Kelly and gives her a hug. She says something in Kelly's ear, and I can see Kelly's red, swollen eyes become redder and fill with moisture.

I reach into my tote bag and grab my portable tissue holder. When April lets go of Kelly and steps back, it's my turn, and I give Kelly a long, tight squeeze. When we pull apart, I hold out the portable tissue holder for her to take, but she reaches into her purse on the top-level of her cart and pulls out her own.

"I came prepared!" She attempts a laugh and dabs at her heavy, tired-looking eyes.

"Megan, I'm sorry I haven't been in touch. I've been meaning to call and thank you for helping me the other night. Everything's been so busy since... I just haven't had time to call anyone."

"Please don't worry about it, Kelly. You're going through so much right now. No one expects you to call or do anything other than take care of yourself. Nothing else matters."

"Everyone in Harmony Lake is thinking of you and hopes you're doing OK. Do you need anything? You only have to ask if you do," April says, choking up at the end of her sentence.

Now we're all crying. It was only a matter of time.

"I'm fine. My sister"—she gestures to her left, where her friend, who I now assume is actually her sister, was standing before she walked away—"and brother-in-law have been amazing. They're really fussing over me, and they've both missed work to help me out. My sister is here with me, but she popped over to the pharmacy to fill a prescription."

"This past week has been so hard…"

Kelly chokes up before she can finish her thought and April and I are both rubbing one of her arms and fighting to keep our own tears from streaming.

I look around and the three of us are alone in the aisle, and I'm aware of what a strange scene this would be to someone else who might come up this aisle. Two emotional women with a bizarre amount of butter are comforting a third, crying woman whose cart is…absolutely full of cleaning supplies? I try not to look shocked when I notice the contents of Kelly's cart.

"Why so many cleaning supplies, Kelly?" I speak softly, trying not to sound critical or judgmental.

If purchasing excessive cleaning supplies is what Kelly needs to do right now to get through this tragedy, then she should do that, and we will support her.

"The police finally released the salon and the apartment, so I'm going over there when we're finished here and plan to spend the rest of today and tomorrow deep cleaning."

She reaches for a box of rubber gloves on the shelf beside her and places them in her cart next to the box of rubber gloves already there.

"There's dust everywhere from fingerprinting and footprints from boots. Everything needs a really thorough scrubbing."

"Do you need any help? I can be a pretty thorough cleaner when I put my mind to it, and Knitorious is closed on Mondays, so I'm free."

"And after I deliver all this butter to the bakery, I can help scrub as long as you need. The three of us could probably get it done pretty quickly," April adds.

"No, thank you, guys. I really want to do this on my own. I'm hoping it'll be cathartic. I plan to go back there on Wednesday after Paul's service and open the salon on Thursday."

"Well, you have my number if you change your mind."

I hope I don't sound relieved. I'm not prepared to go back there today, I'm just not ready. The last place I want to be is at the salon or the apartment above it where I found Paul's body, but I imagine it will be much worse for Kelly. She needs all the support she can get, so I'll suck it up if I have to.

Kelly insists that April and I attend Paul's celebration of life on Wednesday. We ask if we can bring anything or do anything to help, but she says everything is being taken care of, and she wants people to focus on remembering Paul.

"He was such an amazing man. Everyone loved Paul. My voicemail is full of people telling me how much they'll miss him and how generous and kind he was." She tears up and takes a moment to collect herself.

"Harmony Lake definitely won't be the same without him," I say.

It's not a lie. Out of the corner of my eye, I can see April glaring at me.

"He really was one of a kind," April adds.

It's my turn to glare at April.

"I should head to the pharmacy and find my sister." Kelly puts both hands on the handle of her cart in preparation of moving along.

"Before you go…" I reach out and gently place a hand on her cart. "If the police have released the building, does that mean they know who did it? Are they going to arrest someone?"

"They haven't said that, but they don't really tell me anything about the investigation. This Sloane guy likes to ask questions, but he doesn't like to answer them."

So I've noticed.

Kelly's face changes from sad and heavy to frustrated and tense.

"I told him who did it. I told him it's Ryan Wright, but he's still walking around Harmony Lake a free man." She shrugs with both hands in front of her.

"How can you be sure it's Ryan?"

I'm glad April asked, because I wanted to, but held back for fear of upsetting Kelly even more.

Kelly looks at me. "Remember when I told you Paul

thought Ryan wasn't trustworthy and didn't want him in the salon or apartment?"

I nod.

"Well, Ryan tried to talk my Paul into an insurance scam involving the business."

She opens her eyes wide and pauses for a reaction. I open my eyes wide in response and make my best surprised face.

"Ryan said he knows a guy who will pay big money for the new salon equipment. They could make it look like a robbery and I could make an insurance claim to get the stolen equipment replaced. Ryan would give us half of the proceeds of the sale."

"Wow!" I say out loud, even though I meant to say it in my head.

"I know, right?" Kelly says. "I couldn't believe it. I thought Paul misunderstood what Ryan was suggesting, but then he told me that Ryan has done this kind of thing before. Apparently, he went to jail a few years ago for stealing from his employer and re-selling the stolen goods."

"What did Paul say when Ryan suggested this scheme?" April asks, shocked.

"He told Ryan we didn't want anything to do with it and told him if any of my equipment went missing, we'd go straight to the police and tell them it was Ryan who did it."

Paul has a pattern of lying and blackmail, and Ryan has a history that includes time in jail for a similar robbery scheme. Which one of them is lying, and which one is telling the truth?

Kelly and her cart of cleaning supplies make their way toward the pharmacy to find her sister, and April and I and our carts of butter resume shopping and checking items off our lists.

"They don't look alike, do they?" April observes, pointing to Kelly and her sister who are leaving the store with their purchases. "Kelly is blonde and lean, and her sister is brunette and curvy. Like you and me."

"She seems convinced that Ryan killed Paul," I point out.

"She also seems convinced everyone loved him and thought he was a great guy. It was like she was describing a completely different person. Grief must have a way of changing our perspective and making us only remember the parts that we want to remember of the person we lost."

"So is her judgment clouded by grief, or is she blaming Ryan to keep the investigation focused on him and not on her?" I ask rhetorically.

We check out and I follow April to her car so I can transfer the butter from my cart to her trunk.

"Who has a stronger motive," I ask, "Kelly or Ryan?"

"I think it's relative," April replies. "What might not be a big deal to one person might be enough for another person to commit murder."

"And they both have something to gain from Paul's death," I add. "Kelly's business would be protected from Paul's gambling, and Ryan's criminal history would stay a secret."

"But did they both have opportunity?" April asks as

she closes her trunk. "If Archie is telling the truth, Ryan couldn't have done it and only Kelly had the opportunity. She was in the salon while he was right upstairs. She just had to distract Mrs. Pearson long enough to go up there and kill him."

We say good-bye. I walk my cart over to my car, load my groceries in the trunk and head home to take something for the headache I can feel coming on.

CHAPTER 17

I'm walking along Water Street on my way to Knitorious to join Connie. She and I are going together from the store to the Irish Embassy for Paul's celebration of life.

The sunny, warm weather is a stark contrast to the sombre, serious, mood of the town. It's not every day that Harmony Lake buries one of its own, never mind someone as young as Paul or a murder victim.

The WSBA and the town council decided that Water Street businesses could close early today so everyone can attend Paul's celebration of life. The irony of Water Street closing early isn't lost on me. Paul devoted his life to enforcing compliance with every town and WSBA bylaw and ordinance. I don't think he would approve of closing Water Street early on a business day for anyone's funeral, even his own. But, maybe that's the point, to honour Paul in a way that would really mean something to him by changing the rules to accommodate him. Or maybe it's a passive-aggressive way to violate a bunch of bylaws at once since there's nothing Paul can do about it.

It took me a while to decide what to wear. The weather is too fall-like to wear a summer dress and too warm for a winter dress, so I settled on a knee-length, black jersey-knit dress with three-quarter length sleeves, and black calf-high leather boots. I pulled my hair back into a quick French twist and chose not to fight with the few rebellious curls around my face that refused to cooperate.

To add a bit of colour to my all-black ensemble, I switched out my black tote bag for my pumpkin-coloured tote bag. I always carry a tote bag large enough to accommodate my usual purse items along with a knitting project or two, and over the years, I've acquired an impressive collection of them.

Adam texted to say he'll meet Connie and me there because he has an appointment. I heard him on the phone yesterday, and it sounded like he was making arrangements to view an apartment. I'm hoping that's the appointment he has today, and that he likes it, wants to live there and will be telling me soon that he's moving out.

We've decided to start slowly telling our friends and neighbours about our separation after today, so we don't upstage Paul's day. Today, we'll attend the celebration of life together and keep up appearances. We're quite good at that, we've had a lot of practice. The fact that we're arriving separately won't raise any eyebrows because the whole town knows he's a workaholic, and people are used to me arriving at events on my own.

I'm about the reach into my bag for my keys, but I decide to turn the handle and see if the door is already unlocked. It is. I open the door at Knitorious and listen for the jingle above the door. The familiarity makes me feel warm and comfortable. Connie is sitting in the cozy area with Archie Wright and two ladies from the book club.

"Hello, my dear!" Connie waves me over to them. "We're just having a quick cup of tea before we head over. We thought we'd arrive as a group, apparently several community groups are sending a delegation of ambassadors, so we decided we would, too!"

Harlow is curled in a ball and sleeping on her lap.

I greet Connie's friends and make polite small talk while I help to clear the tea cups from the large square coffee table and return them to the sink in the kitchenette.

Our envoy leaves Knitorious, and we walk up Water Street to the crosswalk in front of The Irish Embassy. There are a few people dressed in dark, conservative attire loitering outside the pub entrance, chatting and soaking up the nice weather.

Archie opens the pub door and holds it while the rest of us file past him to enter the building. Or at least we try to enter the building. The pub is completely packed. One step past the doorway and we hit a wall of darkly clad people crammed too close together. Personal space does not exist here, we're literally rubbing shoulders with each other. Well, I'm on the shorter side, so I tend to rub just below the shoulder of most people.

The Irish Embassy is a good-sized pub. It's the equivalent of two of the stores on the north side of Water

Street. The main floor has a long double-sided bar in the centre of the space with stools lining both sides of the bar. The bar also is surrounded by various types of seating, including booths along the walls, tables and chairs in the centre, and a couple of cozy sitting areas with sofas and club chairs around a fireplace. If a dance floor is needed, the tables and chairs can be cleared away to make enough space to dance. There's also room for a band or booth for a DJ.

During tourist season, Sheamus often books local bands for Thursday and Friday nights. It's usually standing room only, but it's still never been as busy as this wake. There's a centre hall staircase immediately behind the bar that leads upstairs where there are two large function rooms, one with a large boardroom-style table and chairs, and one that's empty but can be set up as required. Sheamus' office is also up there, with a couple of extra washrooms, and a large open foyer overlooking the main floor with an intricate wood railing to lean on.

The upstairs is usually closed to the public and available only to private functions renting one of the rooms. Behind the staircase there are more tables and chairs; it's usually quieter behind the stairs than the rest of the pub, so that's a good place to hang out when you want to hear the people you're speaking with. Beyond that is the patio door. The Irish Embassy is one of the few businesses on the south side of Water Street so the patio overlooks the park and the water. It's a beautiful place to spend a summer evening. The patio has tables, chairs, umbrellas, and if there's a live band, the music is piped out to the patio with speakers.

"Wow!" I say as I turn to look at Connie.

"He was young, and involved in every committee, club, cause, and group in town." She shrugs. "I was expecting a full house, but I never imagined it would be like this!"

We suck in our shoulders and try to make ourselves as small as possible to move through the crowd.

Luckily, April is tall and easy to spot. I can see the top of her blonde head about ten feet ahead of me.

"Excuse me! Pardon me! Sorry! Can I just squeeze past? Thank you!" I repeat as I navigate through the tightly packed space. I'm regretting my tote bag because of the extra space it's taking up, and I'm temporarily envious of April who never carries a purse, just a wristlet that acts as both a wallet and phone case.

"I made it!" I declare triumphantly, then give April and Tamara a hug. "But I've lost Connie along the way."

I scan the area immediately around us, but can't see Connie. She's been absorbed into the crowd.

We're discussing how packed the pub is and how warm it is with all these people so close to one another when I see the top of Adam's head making its way through the crowd in our direction.

When he reaches us, I squeeze closer to April to help make room for him. He greets April and Tamara each with a hug and cheek kiss. I'm watching them chat and can't help but notice how flattering his tailored suit is, and while he's always been handsome, age and maturity have only increased his attractiveness.

My mother always said a well-tailored suit is to women what lingerie is to men, and she was right. I catch myself giving him an appreciative head-to-toe-glance and feel a twinge of sadness remembering how once upon a time, seeing him dressed up and watching him charm a room would elicit a stronger physical response from me than just an admiring glance. I can't remember the last time my heart skipped a beat, or I felt the flutter of butterflies in my belly with Adam.

I'm trying to figure out the exact moment that everything changed and we stopped being in love, when the person standing behind me and I accidentally bump into each other. We both turn to apologize at the same time, and I see that it's Phillip Wilde, my neighbour at home and at work.

"Hi Phillip. Sorry to bump you. Sometimes the force of the crowd just kind of moves me, you know?"

I smile and place a hand on his shoulder to steady myself against the movement of the crowd. He leans in and we exchange a double cheek kiss.

"I know what you mean," he whispers in my ear because that's how close he is. "It took us twenty minutes to make our way over to Kelly to give our condolences. I don't think I'll last much longer in this suit. It's getting too warm in here with all the people."

He fans his hand in front of his face.

"I hear ya!" I say.

I sympathize with him about the crowd. Being on the

shorter side, crowds always feel overwhelming to me. I feel less visible when I'm surrounded by a lot of people, like I'm being swallowed up.

Suddenly, the atmosphere changes and the crowd loosens up. We're able to spread out a bit, move our elbows and breathe a little more deeply. I stand on my tippy toes to look around the pub.

"Where is Kelly?" I ask Phillip.

Phillip points over his left shoulder, raises his eyebrows and says, "About twenty minutes that way. She's with her sister and brother-in-law near the fireplace. You might be able to get there in ten minutes now that the crowd has eased up, and if you don't run into too many people you know."

"In this town?" I ask jokingly. "Where everyone knows everyone else?"

We laugh and I turn back to Adam, April, and Tamara.

"It looks like Sheamus opened the patio and upstairs," Adam says, looking up and pointing toward the ceiling.

I'm grateful for the extra space. I silently thank Sheamus for relieving the pressure and letting in the fresh air I can feel starting to come through the patio doors. Then I look up to where Adam is pointing and see people spilling into the open area at the top of the stairs. My eyes follow the line of the wooden railing then stop when I see Eric leaning against it, drink in hand, assessing the crowd below. I catch his gaze, smile, and wave. He smiles back and lifts his drink.

Interesting. I guess it makes sense for him to be here, watching and listening. Does that mean the killer might be here, too, blending in with everyone else, pretending to be a grieving friend and neighbour? I shudder and pull myself back to the here and now.

"Now that there's space to move, we should find Kelly," I suggest. "Phillip said she's with her sister and brother-in-law near the fireplace."

I jerk my head in the direction Phillip pointed to earlier. We move single file through the less crowded room, stopping every few feet to say hello to a neighbour, hug a friend, or smile at an acquaintance.

When we get to Kelly, there's a line of people ahead of us waiting to offer their condolences. Even grieving and traumatized she's one of the most beautiful, graceful women I know. It's just who she is. Her blonde hair is pulled into a low bun, and she's wearing a thin, black, long sleeve turtleneck, a pair of high-rise black wide-leg pants and simple black pumps. Her wedding ring and gold stud earrings are her only jewelry. She's not wearing any makeup and her eyes look swollen and red from crying and probably lack of sleep. She looks exhausted. Poor Kelly. She's having the worst week of her life, but she still manages to put on a smile and deal with a town's worth of people who all want a few minutes with her to offer their sympathies.

My heart breaks for her and I feel like a huge jerk. She's obviously devastated about her husband's death, and here I am thinking she could be the person who killed him.

As I watch how gracefully Kelly handles everything going on around her, and admiring her strength, I see a man's hand comes into view. It disappears behind Kelly's upper back and moves up and down in a rubbing motion. My gaze follows the arm to see the rest of the man attached to it.

It's Fred!

Fred Murphy is rubbing Kelly's back.

CHAPTER 18

I LOOK AWAY from Fred long enough to grab April's arm.

"Are you seeing this?!" I ask, trying to whisper but making more of an angry hissing sound.

April looks away from her wife, and her eyes widen when she sees Fred.

"Is that?" April asks incredulously.

"Yup! That's Fred the blackmailer," I say, interrupting her before she can finish her sentence. "Why is he standing with Kelly?"

I should just stop trying to whisper. Subtlety doesn't seem to be an option currently available to me.

"So… if that's Fred, does that mean the woman on the other side of Kelly is his wife, Stephanie?" April asks. "Are Stephanie and Kelly sisters?"

April's head is still facing Fred, but her eyes are looking at me when she speaks, "I'm sure she's the same woman who was with Kelly at the Shop'n'Save, remember?"

Whoa! My mind is blown.

I scan the room for Adam and spot him by the bar talking to Sheamus. Narrowing my eyes on my target, I inhale sharply and walk over there.

"Hi Sheamus," I say, smiling at him while I clench Adam's forearm, "you really have your hands full today. Do you mind if I borrow Adam for a moment?"

I speak quickly, and without waiting for a response, lead Adam to a quiet, less-populated, corner of the pub. I look him in the eye.

"Is that your girlfriend standing next to Kelly Sinclair? Look behind me, eleven o'clock."

Adam looks. He blinks and does a double take, as if he can't believe what he sees. His reaction answers my question; the woman standing next to Kelly is Stephanie Murphy. Stephanie and Kelly are sisters. Fred and Paul are brothers-in-law.

Feeling overwhelmed as I make the connections in my head, I walk to the nearest table and sit down. It's already occupied, but there's an empty chair. I smile at the people already sitting there.

"Do you mind if I just sit for a moment and catch my breath?"

They all say "of course" slightly out of sync and nod and smile. One of them asks me if I need anything.

"Just to rest for a moment, thanks," I reply, smiling.

I fiddle with my ring and observe Stephanie from the safety of the full table.

Stephanie and Kelly aren't alike at all, and I don't just mean their appearance.

Where Kelly is blonde, slender, and graceful, Stephanie is brunette, curvy, and appears uncomfortable greeting people and making small talk.

Where Kelly has beautiful taste and a classic sense of style, Stephanie is wearing a grey pant suit a size larger than her body, cream-coloured blouse and sensible cream flats that are definitely function over style.

Stephanie and I resemble each other more than Stephanie and Kelly do. We're close to the same height, have curly brown hair, fair skin, and a similar body type with a good helping of boobs and hips, and a small waist. It's kind of creepy that we look alike. Maybe Adam has a type, but this still would make more sense to me if Stephanie bore no resemblance to me.

"I swear, I had no idea they were sisters."

All of a sudden, Adam is standing next to me. I get up, thank the other table occupants, and walk away with Adam following close behind and continuing to speak.

"Honestly, Meg, I didn't even know she was married until Fred contacted me last week, never mind knowing anything about her extended family."

He sounds sincere.

"She doesn't wear a ring, she never talks about her family, and there aren't any photos or personal items in her office. I admit I know she has a cat. She talks about the cat and has photos of him on her phone, but she's never mentioned a husband."

I nod, looking past him at the condolence line.

"But it certainly makes sense now why Kelly didn't want to meet me near my office," he adds.

I glance at Stephanie's ring finger. He's telling the truth; she isn't wearing a ring or any jewelry at all now that I'm looking specifically for jewelry.

She might not have any photos in her office, but Adam does. He framed a photo we took of the three of us at Hannah's graduation ceremony and took it to work for his desk. Stephanie probably recognized me from the photos in his office and that's why she walked away when we made eye contact at the Shop'n'Save on Monday.

"She knew she was married, and you both knew that you were married, even if it is in name only," I say.

Maybe next time, he'll ask more questions before he gets in bed with someone and sends them compromising photos.

"You also knew that you were a partner, she was a junior associate, the relationship was against company policy, not to mention unethical, and put your livelihood and our family at risk," I admonish.

We stand in silence while I collect myself, and he gets over the shock of his wife and girlfriend being in the same room at the same time.

"We should say hello to Kelly and give our condolences," I finally say as I turn and walk toward the condolence line.

April and Tamara go first. I watch as April introduces herself to Fred as though they've never met before and shakes his hand.

Well played, April.

Watching them shake hands reminds me that I should pick up more of those portable hand sanitizer bottles for my purse. It's almost cold and flu season. I'm about to reach into my tote and rifle around for a bottle, so I can use it before and after I shake Fred and Stephanie's hands, but Tamara moves on to talk to Kelly, and it's my turn to greet Fred.

Following April's lead, I shake his hand, fake-introduce myself as a friend of Kelly's and tell him I'm sorry for his family's loss. He fake-introduces himself as Fred, Paul and Kelly's brother-in-law, and thanks me for coming. I tell him that Kelly mentioned how supportive he and his wife have been this past week while silently hoping he feels awkward with all this pretending, because I know I do.

Tamara moves along to Stephanie, so I move along to Kelly, while wiping the hand that touched Fred on my dress.

I hug Kelly and tell her to call, text, or show up anytime day or night if she needs anything. I tell her the town already feels different without Paul. It's not a lie.

I move along to Stephanie and extend my hand for her to shake. Her handshake is weak and limp, and when she tries to end the handshake, I tighten my grip just enough to stop her from pulling her hand away. Then I place my other hand over our conjoined hands.

"I've heard *so much* about you," I say.

I finally let Stephanie pull her hand away from mine. She looks uncomfortable. Good. Though I get the feeling she's uncomfortable generally. Blackmailing witch.

"Kelly says you've been really amazing this week. She's so lucky to have you. She says you and Fred have even taken time off work to support her. What is it you do again?"

I maintain eye contact, and when she averts her eyes, I move my head to compel her to look me in the eye again, engaging her in some kind of weirdly passive-aggressive staring contest I'm determined to win. I think I've even stopped blinking.

"I'm an attorney," she replies.

Even her voice is weak and mousey.

"Right! I remember now," I say, still maintaining eye contact.

I force myself to fake-smile and summon the most chipper sounding voice I have.

"I think you know my husband, Adam Martel!"

I turn to Adam who is just finishing his conversation with Kelly.

"Adam, you know Stephanie, right? You both work at the same firm, I think?"

I look back at Stephanie.

"I'm sorry, I meant to say *worked*. Adam left the firm last week, but I'm sure you know all about that."

I pause to let her squirm, then continue. "Such a small world! Stephanie, we're so sorry for your family's loss," I say, mustering my most consoling tone of voice and tilting my head.

I walk away watching Adam and Stephanie's interaction closely. I don't see any sparks or chemistry between them. If there's still any attraction, it's not palpable. In fact, from where I'm standing, their conversation looks downright awkward, but that could be the result of the scene I just made. They shake hands, and he walks away. I hope their exchange was as uncomfortable for them as it looked.

"What was that, Meg?" Adam asks.

"I'm sorry," I respond. "I've never met my husband's girlfriend before. I don't know what etiquette is correct in this situation. *Please forgive me.*"

I say the last three words with extra sarcasm. I look away from him because I'm fighting the urge to yell and say things I know I'll regret. I walk closer to where April and Tamara are standing.

"Stop calling her my girlfriend. She's not my girlfriend," Adam says.

I look at him, and he rolls his eyes, which only makes me more frustrated.

"Mistress? Concubine? Significant other? What label do you two prefer?" I ask. "Is it awkward having your wife and girlfriend in the same room?"

"I'm going to the bar to get a drink and give you some space. I'll get you a drink, too. You need one," he says calmly.

He turns to April and Tamara, "Ladies, can I get you anything from the bar?"

While avoiding looking at Adam, I notice an elderly couple approach Kelly with a plate of food and motion for her to sit on one of the sofas by the fireplace.

The woman puts the plate down in front of Kelly and begins cutting the food into bite size pieces. Recognizing a mom-move when I see one, I realize the elderly couple are Kelly's parents.

The family settles in the sitting area by the fireplace. Then Fred leans over to Stephanie, says something in her ear, and she nods. Fred gets up, slips away from his in-laws, and heads toward the door with me right behind him.

CHAPTER 19

As I FOLLOW Fred past the bar, I see Adam, and when we make eye contact, I say, "Stay here," silently, exaggerating each word so he can read my lips.

I follow Fred outside and onto the sidewalk in front of the pub. He turns the corner and disappears beside the building, so that's what I do, too.

When I round the corner, his back and his left foot are leaning against the brick wall of the pub, his head is down, his left hand is cupping the lighter in his right hand, and he's lighting the cigarette he's gripping between his lips.

"Filthy habit," I say to let him know I'm here.

He looks at me, pulls a pack of cigarettes from his shirt pocket and extends his arm toward me, silently offering me one. I raise my hand in a stop gesture and shake my head no. I take a step closer, but make sure I'm still visible from the sidewalk, so if I scream someone can see me.

"So, you're Paul's brother-in-law. I didn't see that coming."

He exhales a cloud of smoke.

"I assumed you knew," he says, "Doesn't everyone in this town know everything about everyone else?"

I used to think so, but the past seven days have taught me that there are a lot of secrets in Harmony Lake, and I'm happier not knowing most of them.

"Well, you don't live in this town. I'd never seen you before the day you showed up to blackmail me. I saw you arguing with Paul in a car the day he died, and I did mention that to the police. Why did you give Paul the photos? So, he could blackmail us, too?"

"I didn't blackmail you. I blackmailed Adam," Fred clarifies.

He takes a long drag from his cigarette.

"Same thing," I point out.

"I didn't give Paul the pictures. We didn't know how he got them until after he died. Steph texted Kelly and told her about the affair the day before Paul died and sent the pictures to her. Kelly told the police she thinks Paul found the pictures when he was nosing around her phone and stole them. Steph didn't tell Kelly who the guy in the picture was, only that it was a guy from work," He chuckles. "You should've seen her face when she found out it was your husband."

Fred chuckles again and slaps his knee, then looks at me without turning his head towards me.

So how did Paul know it was Adam in the photos? He might have recognized Adam's tattoo, but I'm not sure he's ever seen it. More likely, he knew Adam and Stephanie worked together and took a stab in the dark that it was Adam. Then Adam inadvertently confirmed it by not denying it was him in the photos when Paul sent them to him and demanded cash.

"I would never give the pictures to him. He's sneaky. He'd find a way to use them for his benefit." He flicks the ash off the tip of his cigarette. "Do you think I want the world to know my wife slept with your husband? If Paul knew and had the pictures to prove it, that's what would have happened, the whole world would know because of him. At least now that he's dead I don't have to deal with him or his problems anymore."

He takes another deep drag from what's left of the cigarette.

"What were you and Paul arguing about in the car?" I ask.

I have nothing to lose by asking. This could be the only chance I get to question Fred, so I should ask all my questions now, while he's talkative.

"Paul owes me money. He told me he would pay me back by blackmailing Adam with the pictures. I was angry that he had the pictures and wanted him to delete them and pretend he never saw them. But Paul's greedy and there's no way he'd delete them if he could use them to squeeze money out of someone."

Fred says all of this matter-of-factly, like he has nothing to hide, then he flicks the cigarette butt into the distance, and we watch it disappear.

Paul told Jay he got the money to repay the loan from his brother-in-law, and Fred just confirmed that Paul owed him money. This statement to Jay might be the only truthful thing I can confirm Paul saying.

"If he owes you money, why kill him? He can't pay you back if he's dead."

I take a step backwards in case Fred freaks out about being accused of murder, and I need to run.

"I didn't kill Paul, but I've been tempted more than once, trust me," he answers, shaking his head. "I was sound asleep when Kelly called from the police station to tell us what happened. I was so tired from the previous two days. Learning about Steph's affair, talking with her to try to save our marriage, dealing with you and Adam, and arguing with Paul made me so exhausted, I passed out right after dinner and slept like I was in a coma. I was so out of it, Steph had a hard time waking me up to go to the police station, and she had to drive because I kept nodding off."

He uses his left foot to push himself away from the wall and stands with both feet on the ground, facing me.

"Look, I don't like Paul and I don't trust Paul, but Kelly loves him, and I love her like a sister. I love my wife and it hurts her when Kelly suffers, so I would never do that to them. And honestly, I never expected Paul to pay me back. He was kind of spiralling financially before he died." He twirls his index finger down in a circular motion. "In fact, he's still costing me money even in death."

Fred chuckles and coughs a phlegmy smoker's cough.

"How is your dead brother-in-law costing you money?" I ask.

"Who do you think is paying for all this?" he answers

my question with a question. "Kelly can't afford this spread. She also can't cover the cost of the funeral or cremation. Steph and I are footing the bill. When I heard he died, I thought, at least his life insurance would cover his final expenses, but we found out yesterday he let the premiums lapse almost a year ago. Kelly has nothing but the business and the contents of the apartment."

With that, Fred walks past me, rounds the corner, and goes back into the pub.

I follow him around the corner and lean against the wall next to the pub door for a minute to process everything Fred just told me before I go back inside.

Instead of crossing suspects off the list, I've found more reasons to keep everyone on the list. First Ryan, with his robbery scheme, criminal history, and revolving door of alibis; then Kelly who wants to protect her home and business from her husband's financially destructive behaviour, and maybe stop him from checking her text messages and calendar entries; and Fred, who admits he hated Paul, was angry because Paul might expose Stephanie's affair with Adam and was tired of bailing him out financially.

And, as much as I hate to admit it and find it impossible to believe, I have to put my own feelings aside and admit that Adam belongs on the list with them. He was being blackmailed by Paul, and he didn't come home the night Paul was killed. He'd already lost his job because of this affair, so maybe being blackmailed for cash on top of that was too much and it pushed him over the edge.

I take a deep breath and go back inside. Adam is

standing just inside the door on the left and Eric is on the right. I avoid looking at Eric because I'm angry at him right now. He knew Kelly and Stephanie were sisters and never mentioned it. He literally stood by and watched while I was blindsided. Again. It's like watching people (me, specifically) squirm is his hobby, or something.

I accept the glass of Pinot from Adam and take a long sip.

"Are you OK?" Adam asks. "I worried when he came back in and you didn't. I was about to come looking for you."

"I'm more confused than before I spoke to him, but other than that I'm fine," I mumble.

I take a deep breath and repeat, "heavy shoulders long arms," a few times in my head to help release the tension in my neck and shoulders.

Out of the corner of my eye, I see flailing arms. April is trying to get my attention. Now that the crowd is starting to thin out, she, Tamara, and Connie were able to claim a booth.

Adam and I join them. I sit down, put my tote on the floor under the booth and fill them in on my conversation with Fred.

April and I are both in awe of Kelly's lying skills. When we saw her at the grocery store on Monday, she didn't let on that she knew about Stephanie and Adam. Also, neither of us recall her referring to her sister by name, just as "my sister," and I'm wondering if that was intentional. But then she insisted I come to the celebration of life today, so she must have known I'd find out her sister and Stephanie

Murphy are the same person. Maybe I'm over thinking it. She could be so deeply mired in her own grief that lying to me or covering for her sister's bad decisions isn't even on her radar right now.

"Well, either she's grieving and doesn't care, or she's an academy award worthy actor," Connie observes.

"Paul was going through Kelly's phone? Maybe she found out and got angry. Or maybe she found out that he was blackmailing Adam and threatening to expose her sister in the process, and it pushed her over the edge," Tamara surmises.

It certainly does seem like there were trust issues in Paul and Kelly's marriage, at least on his part. Especially when he found out that Kelly was texting and meeting with Adam in the summer. I'm careful not to share this bit of information with anyone else because Adam told me in confidence. The only person he told, aside from me, is Eric Sloane. If only he were as discreet with his personal relationships as he is with his professional ones, we wouldn't be tangled up in this tangled yarn of a murder investigation.

"Until today, I thought Fred was the least likely suspect because Paul owed him money and it's hard to collect a debt from a dead man, but today Fred said he wasn't expecting Paul to pay him back. Also, until yesterday, the family thought Paul was insured, but they found out he stopped paying the premiums almost a year ago. So, maybe he killed Paul for the insurance and it backfired," I suggest.

"I think Fred is the strongest contender for the title of

Killer," April says. "If we were betting, I'd put my money on him."

"I don't know." I bite the inside of my lip while I wrestle with the gut feeling that Fred didn't do it. "He kept referring to Paul in the present, you know? Like he said 'I *don't* like Paul. Paul *owes* me money. He *is* sneaky. Wouldn't the killer use past tense? And he didn't hesitate to talk to me, like he has nothing to hide."

Or maybe he's just fed up with being suspected of murder and wants to wrap this up already. If that's the case, I can relate because I feel the same way; this would be the only thing Fred Murphy and I have in common.

"We know he's capable of blackmail, and lying, so how big of a leap is it to murder someone?" Connie theorizes.

Everyone shrugs and nods their heads. I'm conflicted. Logically, I know Fred is a strong suspect, but my instincts don't agree.

"Are you ready to head out?" Adam asks me.

"I think I'll stay and have another glass of wine. Then I'll walk Connie home. So, I'll see you at home," I say, smiling at him.

"Meg, there's a murderer in our midst and you're asking questions and trying to figure out who it is. You could be putting yourself in danger. I'd feel better if I walk you and Connie home."

He's laying out his argument using his lawyer voice, and I hate it when he uses his lawyer voice to argue with me.

"I'll be fine, Adam. You can go ahead and leave. I'll text

you when I'm on my way. You don't have to worry," I insist and wave him away dismissively.

"Archie and some of the book club are coming back to the shop for tea after, so I won't be alone anyway, but thank you, Adam."

Connie reaches over and squeezes his hand.

"I'll make sure she gets home safely," Eric says, now standing beside the booth. "Megan, I'd like to speak with you before you leave. Then I can make sure you get home safely, if that's all right."

"Sure," I say.

I look at Adam. "See, I'll be fine. I'll see you at home."

Adam says goodbye to the table, thanks Eric, and leaves.

"I'll be sitting by the bar when you're ready," Eric says, and turns to walk toward the bar.

"Megan? Why are you Megan, and T and I are Ms. Shaw, and Ms. Shaw"?

"Dunno, he told me to call him Eric, so I told him to call me Megan."

"I really need to figure out who killed Paul so everything can go back to normal, and I can get on with my life," I say.

"Are you sure going back to normal is what you want, my dear? Everything to be exactly as it was?"

Connie places her hand on top of mine and gives it a gentle squeeze.

"I'm going to get us another round of drinks. Or possibly two!" April announces.

CHAPTER 20

WITH A SLIGHT BUZZ from having three glasses of wine over the course of the afternoon and no food, I wander over to the bar and find Eric sitting on a bar stool with a plate of wings and a drink that I assume is non-alcoholic because police on TV never drink while they're on duty.

"Is that from the local microbrewery?" I point to his pint glass.

"Only if the local microbrewery brews ginger ale," he replies, smiling. "Wing?"

He nudges a plate of wings toward me. I put a hand up and shake my head to indicate no thank you and sit on the stool next to him at the now almost-empty bar.

"I can't believe how busy it was in here earlier. I've never seen so many people crammed into The Embassy," I say, making an attempt at small talk.

"It was crazy," he agrees. "It made it difficult to observe everyone. But I observed you racing out of here after Fred. How did that go?"

He gets right to the point. All business, this guy.

"I'm sure he didn't tell me anything that you don't already know. Like how you already knew that Stephanie and Kelly are sisters and that Stephanie and Fred would be here today, and I didn't."

It's a relief to get this off my chest. One of the many, many things I've learned over the last week is that I need to speak up when I'm upset and not shove my feelings aside. It's not my job to spare other people from having uncomfortable feelings at the expense of my own. I deserve to be heard, too, everybody does. As of today, I promise myself I will say how I feel and not ignore my feelings for the sake of not rocking the boat.

I will keep this promise at least until this wine buzz wears off.

"Actually, until I saw the look on your face when you saw them, I didn't know you weren't aware of the relationships there. Harmony Lake is a small town, everyone seems to know everyone else, so I assumed you knew. I'm sorry that was awkward for you, it wasn't my intention."

I guess he didn't blindside me intentionally.

"Thank you," I reply. "Why were you watching me?"

"I wasn't watching *you* specifically. I was watching the condolence line. It was so busy in here that I had to narrow my focus, so I kept an eye on the condolence line from upstairs while a few non-uniforms wandered the crowd with their eyes and ears open," he explains.

While Eric finishes his wings and ginger ale, I fill him in on my conversation with Fred and share the conclusions that Connie, April, Tamara, and I came to when we discussed it earlier.

"I really appreciate the information, it's more helpful than you realize, but Adam is right to be concerned about your safety. There is a murderer in this town, and they probably know that you're asking questions and talking to me. If that person thinks you're getting too close, you could be in danger. I think it's time for you to stop investigating and go back to your normal life."

I feel like he's being sincere, and not just trying to get my nose out of his case, though I'm sure that's part of it.

"I need this murder to be solved because Adam and I are suspects. We have a daughter, and I don't want her to think that her father had an affair with a married woman, we were blackmailed because of it, and one of us killed his blackmailer. Even part of it being true is bad enough, but it will be easier to explain to her when someone else is behind bars for Paul's murder," I explain. "Adam is a lawyer and that's how we support our family. Being a suspect in a murder investigation could destroy his career. I mean, would you hire a lawyer who may have killed the person who was blackmailing him? The affair has already cost him his partnership at the firm."

I'm getting choked up, and I can feel my cheeks flushing. Talking about how this would affect Hannah makes it too real. I take a deep breath, dab my eyes with a napkin from the bar and compose myself.

"If I tell you something, can you promise me that you won't tell another person?" Eric asks quietly.

He makes a fist and extends his pinky finger for a pinky swear. I hook my pinky finger around his.

"Promise," I say.

Then I use my other hand to make an X over my heart.

"I pinky swear and I cross my heart and hope to die, so spill."

"Adam has been eliminated as a suspect. We were able to use video and his key card for the office building to verify he arrived at work early in the morning and didn't leave his office until late Tuesday evening. From there he went to a burrito place up the street. We have video of him ordering food, leaving with his order, and entering a nearby hotel a few minutes later. We have proof that he registered and was given a key card for the company suite. We have footage of him and his burrito entering the elevator, then exiting on the floor where the suite is located. We have video of him unlocking the door with the key card. The door to that suite wasn't opened again until the next morning. He couldn't have done it."

I tear up from the overwhelming relief I feel.

"Well…" I sigh. "At least with Adam eliminated, if I go to prison for Paul's murder, Hannah will still have one parent on the outside."

When I hear the words come out of my mouth, I realize I sound glib, but I'm seriously worried that I haven't been eliminated as a suspect yet, and other people have, which means the suspect list is getting smaller and my odds of being charged are getting higher.

"As for you," Eric says, handing me another napkin, "you were at work until less than ten minutes before you found the body, and you were with Connie all afternoon before that. While you haven't been eliminated, you are, at best, an unlikely suspect."

I nod. An unlikely suspect, but a suspect nonetheless.

"I was planning to stop by tomorrow and tell Adam, but we can tell him when I take you home if you want."

I nod. "That would be great, thank you, Eric."

"So, there's no need for you to keep asking questions and putting yourself at risk, right?" he nods at me, looking for agreement.

"Right," I say, nodding back.

We get up to leave. We say goodnight to Sheamus and head toward the door.

"Thank you for offering to take me home, but you don't have to," I say. "I'll be fine, really."

"I don't doubt it," he says, "but it's a good idea for everyone to be extra cautious right now, and go out in groups and pairs. You know, safety in numbers and all that. Besides, I promised your hus—Adam, and this gives me a chance to tell him he's no longer a suspect."

At the door, I reach for my tote to get my lip balm. Where's my tote bag?

"Shoot! I left my bag under the booth!"

I walk quickly toward the booth and can see my pumpkin-coloured bag underneath the table where I left it. I reach under, grab it, stride back to Eric, through the door he's holding open, and onto the sidewalk, completely forgetting that my lips are dry and I wanted to apply lip balm.

Eric doesn't have a car with him. He rode to The

Embassy with two non-uniformed colleagues who left long ago and took the car with them. It's a nice evening, so we decide to walk to my house and he'll text the station and ask for a patrol car to pick him up.

On the walk to chez Martel, we talk about hockey, we're both Toronto Maple Leaf Fans. We talk about school. I went to U of T, and he went to Laurentian. We talk about TV, we both hate reality shows, I prefer streaming services, he prefers cable. He even answers a few personal questions. I learn he's been divorced for two years after being married for ten to a chiropractor, his job caused stress in their marriage, and he has no children. He doesn't have a girlfriend. He says he's married to his job, and if he tries to have both a relationship and a career, one or the other suffers, so he's given up trying to have both.

When we get to the house, the porch light is on and door is locked. Adam isn't kidding around about our security; we rarely lock the door when one of us is home. I don't like feeling that I have to lock my door to feel safe in my home.

Instead of ringing the bell and disturbing him, I reach into my bag and grope around for my keys. I grab hold of something that feels…odd.

What is this? It's smooth and cylindrical, and Eric and I both watch as I slowly pull a twelve-inch-long, fifteen millimetre diameter, bamboo knitting needle from my bag and hold it up between us.

"What the fff—what is this? This isn't mine. It wasn't in here when I switched bags this morning."

I'm dumbfounded trying to figure out where this knitting needle came from and how it got into my bag.

"Are you sure it's not yours? Maybe it was already in your bag from the last time you used it and you forgot it was there?"

Eric positions his hands cautiously near the needle, being careful not to touch it, like he's prepared to catch it if it falls.

"I'm sure. We sell these at the shop. In fact, this one is identical to the needles that Kelly bought the day Paul died."

I look at his face for a reaction, but he's hyper-focused on the needle I'm dangling between us.

"I don't own needles this big," I explain. "I usually knit with fingering weight or worsted weight yarn so my needle collection ranges from about two millimetres to about five millimetres. Nothing this big, and I only use circular needles, even when I'm knitting flat, so this definitely isn't mine."

He looks at me blankly for a second, then returns his focus to the needle.

"I don't know what any of that means," he says as he presses the doorbell with one hand while continuing to guard the needle with the other, "but that needle might be evidence. I need you to carefully and gently place it back in your bag without touching it any more than you already have."

Adam opens the door, looks at me, looks at Eric, then looks at the needle.

"Hey, guys!" he says with a big smile.

CHAPTER 21

HOLDING my bag at arm's length, I walk briskly from the front door to the dining room and gently, as if my bag contains a grenade and not a bamboo knitting needle, I place the bag on the dining room table and step away backwards, keeping watch over it the entire time.

I switch on the light over the table. I can hear Eric behind me on his phone. He's requesting a car and an evidence kit.

I look at Adam and see he's confused. I tell him about the unexplained knitting needle I found in my bag. He still looks confused, and I realize that after living with a knitter for twenty years, he's used to finding random knitting needles in unexpected places and doesn't think a rogue needle appearing in my tote bag is unusual. I explain to him that this particular needle isn't mine, and Eric thinks it might be evidence. The confused look on his face is replaced with a look of concern.

Eric finishes his call.

"We're going to have to take the entire bag and its contents for processing," he explains.

"Oh…will I be able to keep my cell phone at least? That's the number Hannah uses to reach me."

"Not if it's in your bag, I'm afraid," he responds, shaking his head.

"They'll probably have it for a while," Adam adds. "They still have my cell phone, and it's almost been a week. It might take them a week just to unpack everything from your luggage."

I roll my eyes. Adam always teases me about my love of large tote bags. "Luggage" is one of his many terms of endearment for them. I know he's trying to lighten the mood and ease my anxiety about having my stuff confiscated, but right now I'm not amused.

"It's still pretty early," Adam says, looking at his watch. "If it's all right with Eric that I leave, I'll go to the store and get you a new phone. You can text Hannah with your new number tonight, and if she needs anything in the meantime, she'll text me or call the landline. We'll tell her the phone got wet or something. It'll be fine."

I nod, feeling sad I have to lie to my daughter because I can't tell her that evidence from a murder, that I'm suspected of committing, appeared in the bag that had my cell phone in it and was confiscated by the police.

"Go ahead," Eric says to Adam, "but I'll need to ask you some questions when you get back."

"I'll be as quick as I can."

Adam is already at the door putting on his shoes.

"Would you like a coffee or tea or anything?" I go into

the kitchen to get myself a glass of water, while Eric stays in the dining room with my pumpkin-coloured, vegan-leather tote bag.

"No thanks. So, when was the last time you remember reaching into your bag? Before we got here and you went looking for your keys, I mean."

I think back. I realized I didn't have it when I wanted to put lip balm on as we left the pub. I remember returning to find it under the booth where I had put it when I first sat down. I remember wanting my hand sanitizer in the condolence line but was interrupted because it was my turn to fake-introduce myself to Fred. I didn't need my key to go into Knitorious because the door was unlocked.

"I think the last time was when I left the house this afternoon," I say loudly from the kitchen. "I locked the door and put my keys in my bag. I don't think I've reached into it since. It was under the booth most of the afternoon. When it wasn't under the booth, it was on my shoulder. I switched bags this morning, and I'm telling you, there were no knitting needles in my bag except for the ones that belong in my bag. I have a sock project in there that I keep with me, so I can work on it in line-ups, waiting rooms, you know, when I'm waiting. But it's a sock and has tiny needles."

I take off my boots and put them in the closet by the front door. Then I go into the living room and sit on the sofa with my feet tucked up under my butt. The living room and dining room are attached, and I'm able to position myself with a clear view of the bag on the dining room table.

"Did anyone hold your bag for you?" Eric asks.

"No." I shake my head. "It was on my shoulder or under the booth. Lots of people bumped into it though because the pub was so crowded. Are you going to explain to me how the knitting needle might be evidence?"

"They're here," Eric says, walking to the front door to let in two police officers.

The three law enforcement officers proceed to the dining room, one of them places a black case on the dining room floor. She opens the case, pulls out a pair of latex gloves and puts them on. Then she grabs a large plastic evidence bag which she then unfolds into an even larger evidence bag. She reaches into the case again and pulls out more, smaller evidence bags and lays them neatly in front of her. The other officer reaches into the case and puts latex gloves on. The two officers begin to methodically photograph, bag, and tag the contents of my tote bag. I'm glad Adam isn't here to crack a joke about the size of the evidence bag they need to fit the tote bag inside.

While the bag is being processed, Eric suggests we wait in another room, so I lead him into the family room and resume my tucked-up position on the sofa there. Eric sits down at the other end of the sofa.

"Well," I say, "how is this knitting needle potential evidence?"

Instinctively, I pick up the sock-in-progress from the ceramic yarn bowl on the table next to me and start knitting.

"That's a nice bowl. Did you make that?"

It's like he'll do anything to avoid directly answering my question.

"Thank you. Yes, I took a pottery class a few years ago and made it."

Eric moves closer, so he's in the middle of the sofa instead of the end.

"Remember when I explained to you what a 'hold-back' is?" he asks quietly.

He's speaking so quietly, I have to lean in so I can hear him.

"Yes." I nod. "It's evidence that only the killer would know about. You keep it a secret until you find the killer and can use the holdback to verify their story," I whisper.

"Pretty much," he whispers back. "One of the knitting needles that Kelly bought at Knitorious was missing from the crime scene. We haven't been able to find it anywhere. We turned the apartment, salon, their cars, everything upside down looking for it. One needle was there, but we weren't able to locate the other one."

"So, you think the killer took it? Like a sick souvenir or something?" I ask.

The thought of someone being so disturbed that they would want a memento from a murder scene makes me visibly cringe.

"Possibly," he says, nodding.

He pauses, making me think he's not sure if he should say anything else.

"We also think the needle may have been used as a garrote. Do you know what a garrote is?" he whispers.

I look at him and nod. I feel my stomach sink, and I swallow hard.

I know a garrote is a weapon used to help strangle someone. The police suspect the killer might have used the knitting needle as a tool to tighten the yarn around Paul's neck. I also know its sudden appearance in my bag means I've probably exchanged my status as unlikely suspect for the status of most likely suspect.

"Will you be able to keep this knitting needle a secret, Megan? It would really help the investigation if we could keep it under wraps. I know you're close with April and Connie. Will you be able to keep this from them? The killer probably wants you to find it, and touch it, and I'd rather not give this creep what they want." Eric winks at me. An attempt to be reassuring.

I'm not reassured, I'm terrified. My fingerprints are on that needle, I touched it to pull it out of my bag. The killer probably took it with them after they killed Paul, wiped it clean of their own fingerprints, then planted it in my purse so I could leave my fingerprints on it. This needle directly links me to Paul's murder.

"Of course, I'll keep it a secret." I tell him firmly.

In silence and with trembling hands, I knit while Eric paces back and forth between the officers in the dining room and me in the family room.

Adam comes home with my new phone, hands me the box and I take it into the kitchen to plug it in while he and Eric speak in the family room. The other two officers finish collecting and cataloguing the evidence and pack up their things.

I text Hannah with my new number. I'm waiting for her to text back an acknowledgement and thinking about the knitting needle.

I touched a weapon that was used to murder someone. It was in my bag, and I didn't even realize it was there.

A knitting needle of all things. I love knitting. It has brought me comfort during some of the hardest times of my life, like when my mother passed away. Knitting helped me make friends when we first moved to Harmony Lake, and now knitting might frame me for a murder I didn't commit. I feel gross and dirty and can't wait for the police to leave, so I can lock myself in my room and have a shower.

I'VE BEEN STANDING under the stream of hot water for a long time and the tips of my fingers are wrinkled and pruney.

Does Eric really believe I'm innocent? Does everyone else believe I'm innocent? Why did the killer want me to find the murder weapon, instead of someone else?

This means the murderer was at Paul's celebration of life, walking around, acting normal, and doing it well enough that they didn't stand out.

The water starts to run cold and I shiver. I turn off the water and step out of the shower, into the steam-filled washroom to dry off.

I put on my favourite flannel pyjamas with cats and

yarn on them, a pair of thick, hand-knit, wool socks, and go to the kitchen to make a mug of chamomile tea.

Adam is at the kitchen table with his laptop open.

"Did you text your new number to Hannah?" he asks without looking up from the screen.

"Yes, it's all good. Thank you for replacing my phone."

I feel a lump in my throat and force myself to swallow.

"Do you think I killed Paul?" I blurt out.

Tears well up in my eyes, and I can't stop them from streaming down my face.

Adam gets up from his seat at the table, walks over to the kitchen counter, and picks up a tissue box. He pulls out a couple of tissues, hands them to me, and puts the box on the counter next to me.

"I know you didn't kill anybody. No one who has ever met you could think that you're capable of murder. The real killer must feel cornered and desperate to redirect the investigation," he says, rubbing my back reassuringly.

"Eric seems really thorough, good at his job. I'm sure he's seen this type of thing before, knows you didn't do it, and will find the monster who did."

He puts his arms around me, and I let him. I cry there for a while. At least if I'm charged, I'll have a good lawyer.

After I pull myself together, I make my tea, and say goodnight to Adam.

"Eric spoke to you about keeping the knitting needle a secret, right? It's really important, Meg. If we tell anyone, it could jeopardize the investigation."

He's speaking to me gently now, like he would speak to an upset child.

"I understand. I won't say anything. I can keep a secret you know. I've kept our separation a secret for months."

As soon as I say it, I realize I sound bitter, which isn't my intention.

"He also told me that you've been eliminated as a suspect, and he said he was going to tell you tonight," I tell him.

"He told me, and I know you can keep a secret, but I also know that you confide in your friends, but you can't confide in them about this. Tell them the same story about your phone that you told Hannah. It'll be easier to keep track of the lies if we keep them consistent," he says, smiling at me. "Goodnight."

He sits down at the kitchen table and resumes working on his laptop.

I've become a person who has enough lies that she has to keep track of them. I need to solve this murder so I don't have to lie anymore.

This isn't who I am.

CHAPTER 22

I didn't sleep well. During the short time I did sleep, I dreamt I was in prison with the cast of Orange Is The New Black.

After tossing and turning for the rest of the night, I'm wide awake so I may as well get up, get dressed, and go to Knitorious, ship the online orders that have come in since the last time I shipped online orders, and maybe work on the fall window display.

Realizing that my keys were one of the items confiscated with my tote bag last night, I retrieve the spare set of keys from the hook on the wall in the laundry room and drive to the store.

I park in the back and quietly let myself in through the back door. I don't want to use the front door because the bell might wake up Connie, and no one should have to be up this early if they don't have to be.

Harlow runs downstairs and purrs while he wraps

himself around my ankles. I pick him up, scratch under his chin, tell him how charming he is, and carry him into the store. I sit on one of the sofas and he jumps onto my lap. I stroke him, he purrs, and we enjoy the quiet time together until he purrs himself to sleep.

I pick up the cowl I'm working on to knit for a while before I print the online orders. The clicking of the needles and Harlow's purring are the only sounds in the otherwise silent store. For the first time in over a week I feel anxiety loosening its grip on me, and I'm grateful for the break, even if it's only for a few minutes.

Harlow wakes up, licks himself, and leaps off my lap. He's meowing and looking back and forth between me and the kitchenette.

"Are you hungry, handsome?" I ask him.

I stand up and he runs toward the kitchenette. While doling out his pungent food, I hear footsteps behind me on the stairs to Connie's apartment.

"Good morning, sleepy head!" I say to Connie, without turning around.

I put Harlow's dish down on the floor and turned to look at Connie.

"Oh!" I gasp, "Where's Connie?"

"Good morning, Megan! Connie will be down in a minute. We didn't think you were coming in this morning," Archie replies.

This is awkward for both of us. I had no idea Connie and Archie were more than friends, or that they have sleepovers. I wonder if this has anything to do with the mystery appointments she's been having lately.

I try to act like it's totally normal for Archie to do a walk of shame out of Connie's apartment on a Thursday morning.

"How are you doing, Archie? How's that sore hip been treating you?"

I hold up a coffee mug to offer him a cup of coffee.

"It's stiff, but as long as I keep using it, it's OK. It's when I stop using it that it seizes up, so I try to keep it moving" he replies, shaking his head and waving away my offer of a cup of coffee. "Listen, Megan, I was talking with Connie, and she mentioned that Ryan might have misinformed you about where he was the night Paul died."

"I was wondering about that," I say, turning the coffee machine on.

"Well, it's true that we watched the game together that night, but before that, he wasn't with his friend Jay, he was with me. He was caught off guard, you see, and he didn't know what to say. He was protecting me as much as he was protecting himself."

"Just tell her, Archie!" Connie is coming down the stairs now, and I sense this morning-after scene isn't about to get less awkward.

"Good morning, my dear." Connie and I hug, and she kisses my cheek.

"Stop beating around the bush, Archie, and tell her where you were," she says, taking his hand.

Archie takes a deep breath.

"Ryan and I were at an AA meeting at a church in Harmony Hills. He got his three-year chip that night."

"Archie, I had no idea! Good for him. Tell Ryan I'm proud of him. Sobriety isn't easy. And please tell him that his secret is safe with me. I won't tell a soul," I reassure him.

"Us," Archie corrects me. "We were both at the meeting, Megan. I've been sober for 23 years."

He smiles at me and then at Connie.

"Like father, like son," Archie says, "I'm afraid my rugged good looks and seductive charm aren't the only things I've passed down to my son."

Connie laughs and puts her spare hand on his shoulder.

"Ryan was taken aback when you asked him where he was, and he didn't want to out my sobriety. That's why he lied to you. He feels awful for lying. He was with me the entire night, I swear."

"I'm proud of both of you." I hug him. "And I couldn't be happier for you and Connie. Actually, I feel better knowing that you're staying here while there's a killer roaming around Harmony Lake."

I finish making my coffee, say goodbye to Archie and go into the shop to print the online orders. Connie and Archie say their goodbyes at the back door, then she joins me in the shop.

Connie looks happy. There's no denying that she has a glow and a spring in her step that I haven't seen since her husband passed almost five years ago. Archie obviously makes her happy, and that's enough to make me happy for them.

"I mean it, you know," I say. "I really am happy for you and Archie. But why the secrecy?"

"It's not a secret. We just didn't announce it. We decided to live our life and let people figure it out for themselves. Making a big deal out of it at our age sounds exhausting, to be honest, and as soon as the right people figure it out, it will be common knowledge anyway." She shrugs, smiles, and starts tidying up skeins of yarn on the shelves behind the sofa.

While processing the online orders, I think about what Connie said about her relationship with Archie becoming common knowledge. Until last week, I thought that nothing could stay secret for long in Harmony Lake, but this past week, I've realized that no matter how small the town and how tight knit the community, there are secrets lurking in everyone's lives. Even our family has a secret, and if we can keep a separation secret for months, anyone can do it. I feel like I don't know anybody as well as I thought I did.

Connie and I both look up at the door when we hear the familiar jingle of the bell. April walks in with a deep frown.

"There you are!" she shouts at me. "I've been texting you all day. I was worried, so I texted Adam to make sure you were OK. He said you have a new phone number and that I'd probably find you here. What happened to your phone, and why are you here on your day off?"

"What's this about a new number, my dear?"

Now, Connie has a concerned look on her face.

"I'm sorry! I meant to text you both with my new

number, but I don't actually *know* your phone numbers. I'm so dependent on technology now, that I don't have anyone's contact information written down anywhere."

I make a mental note to get one of those old-timey phone books and write down important numbers, in case I ever have another phone confiscated by the police or actually do ruin it by getting it wet.

"The phone is no big deal, I dropped it in water last night after the celebration of life and it didn't recover. I was worried Hannah wouldn't be able to reach me, so Adam went out and replaced it."

I smile and look back and forth from April to Connie, hoping they believe me and hating that I just lied to them. Not telling them something would be bad enough, but this is an outright lie.

"As for coming in on my day off, there are online orders that need to go out, the fall window isn't finished, and honestly, being home is awkward right now with my soon-to-be-ex-husband there all the time, you know?"

The last part isn't a lie, it is awkward with Adam being at home so much. We seem to always be in each other's space.

Connie walks over to the counter with her right hand extended, palm-up. Wiggling her fingers, she says, "Give me your phone and I'll text myself, so we have each other's numbers. I agree with April, I would've panicked if I tried to reach you and couldn't. We still have a killer roaming around, remember?"

I unlock my new phone and hand it to Connie who, despite claiming not to understand anything technological, is able to find the text app, text herself, then hand the phone back to me. I hold the phone out to April who takes it and adds her and Tamara's numbers.

"Why were the police at your house last night?" April asks. "Phillip said there were two patrol cars, and they were there for a while."

Uh-oh, Adam and I didn't come up with a lie to explain why the police were at the house. I wonder if Phillip saw the evidence bags that they took to their cars.

"Eric walked me home after the celebration of life and his colleagues came to pick him up."

It's not an outright lie. I know I'm lying by omission, but it feels less awful than saying something that's completely untrue.

"Phillip said there were two cars," April says, holding up two fingers, "Eric needs two cars to drive him around?"

April raises her eyebrows, tilts her head, and crosses her arms in front of her chest. She obviously isn't buying it. Connie stands next to her in some kind of show of solidarity, crossing her arms in front of her chest, too.

"Ok, Eric really did need a ride back to the station, that's true. He also spoke to Adam to let him know that he's been eliminated as a suspect...and... he called a couple of officers to come in and pick up.... some.... evidence...that may have appeared suddenly yesterday."

"Keep talking, my dear," Connie says, moving her hand in a rolling motion in front of her.

"I really want to tell you, but I can't. Eric said the entire investigation could be compromised. Please stop asking because I want to tell you, but I can't. And, please don't mention this to anyone."

I bring my palms together, in a pleading motion in front of my face.

"Of course, we won't say anything! We know you'd tell us if you could. Let's just hope whatever it is, it breaks the case wide open and gets this murderer off our streets."

"Your secrets are always safe with us, my dear." Connie says as she wraps her arms around both of us and gives us a big squeeze.

"Now that we've sorted that out," April says, "Latte Da's fall menu starts today and I'm craving a spiced caramel apple latte. Come with me, and we can see what other fall yummies they've added to their menu this year."

April is rubbing her tummy in a circular motion. As much as I love coffee, April loves it more. Her commitment to it is admirable. Coffee is kind of her hobby.

"Give me five minutes to finish packing this order, so I can drop these off at the post office on our way."

I start placing the packaged orders into a large reusable laundry bag with a pink and brown tartan pattern.

"That laundry bag is almost as big as your purse!" April says, pointing at the large bag, laughing, and looking at Connie who's covering her mouth with her hand to hide her laughter.

"Ha! Ha!" I say, "Everyone likes to make fun of my bag until they need me to carry something for them, don't they, April?"

I look up at April without lifting my head from the order I was packing. April only carries a wristlet, which is a combination of her phone case and wallet, so whenever we go anywhere together, she puts whatever didn't fit in her wristlet—which is basically everything—in my tote. At any given time, up to half of the things in my bag actually belong to her.

My cell phone dings:

Adam: Can you meet me at 845 Mountain Road at 1pm? I want to show you something

Me: Yes! C u there!

I'm so excited, I almost add a smiley emoji to the end of my text reply to him.

"I don't want to jinx it, but I think Adam found an apartment," I say. "I heard him on the phone the other day and it sounded like he was setting up a viewing. He just texted me asking if I would meet him at 845 Mountain Road at 1 p.m."

I'm grinning so wide my cheeks hurt, and I do a little happy dance behind the counter.

"Mountain Road...those are mostly older houses, right? Some have been converted to duplexes and triplexes, I think? And a few have been renovated to be businesses? A bit off the beaten path, but nice and close to the highway." April nods.

"That reminds me." Connie snaps her fingers and interjects, "I have an appointment tomorrow, late morning. Will you be OK here by yourself for a couple of hours?"

"Of course," I tell her. "Is everything OK, Connie? You've had several appointments over the last few weeks, should we be worried?"

Scared the answer might be yes, I brace myself. Connie

is like a mother to me, and I can't imagine anything happening to her. Also, I can see she's starting to slow down a bit.

"Nothing to worry about, my dear." She waves her hand dismissively. "At my age a few extra appointments are to be expected," she adds with a wink at me.

"Promise you'd tell us if something was wrong?" April extends her pinky finger to Connie for a pinky swear, and Connie, hooking her own pinky finger around April's says, "pinky swear, my dear."

CHAPTER 23

IN UNISON, April and I move our sunglasses from the tops of our heads to our eyes as we step out of the post office and onto the sunny sidewalk. We walk in the direction of Latte Da and enjoy the sun on our faces while I fill April in about Ryan being off their suspect list, without disclosing where Ryan and Archie were the night Paul was murdered. Besides, April forgets all about Ryan and his alibi when I tell her about running into Archie on his way out of Connie's apartment this morning.

"Just wow!" April's mouth is open in disbelief. "I mean, good for them. They're both such great people, and they deserve to be happy, but it's shocking that we live in such a small town, and we're so close with Connie, yet we never knew."

"I know," I agree with her. "I've been thinking the same thing lately. We assume because we're in a small town where everybody knows one another, that it's hard to keep a secret, but since Paul died, all we've done is find out people's secrets. It makes me wonder how well we can really know anyone."

"Well, you know me as well as anyone can!" April pulls the door to Latte Da and motions for me to go ahead of her. "And I have no secrets. What you see is what you get."

She lets the door close behind her and joins me in line. Latte Da is busy today. Everyone is here checking out the new fall menu, making sure their favourite fall drink is back, and looking to see what new items have been added.

We order our coffees and sit in the last available cozy sitting area in the coffee shop. I put my mocha chip iced coffee on the table, settle into my seat and pull out my knitting. I want to finish Hannah's cowl and hat before she comes home for Thanksgiving in October. I'm also hoping this murder investigation is solved by then, so Hannah won't come home to a mother who is a murder suspect. Tears began to well up in my eyes, thinking about Hannah and what could happen if the killer isn't found.

"Hey…" April touches my knee. "Are you OK? You aren't listening to my review of this Spiced Caramel Apple Latte, or if you are, it's so boring it's bringing you to tears."

"I'm sorry," I put my knitting on my lap. "I'm worried because Hannah will be home for Thanksgiving in three weeks and I'm still a murder suspect. We haven't even told her about the investigation. She has no idea I'm a suspect or that Adam was a suspect. I just want it solved so badly."

A familiar voice gets my attention, and I look toward

the cash register to see Kelly paying for her order. Hairway to Heaven is right next door, so it makes sense to run into her here. Kelly looks over and sees me looking at her. She starts waving.

"Hey ladies!" she calls. "Save me a seat. I'll join you as soon as my Gingerbread Spiced Coffee is ready."

I wave back at her and nod.

"I still have feelings about her knowing about Adam and Stephanie, and not saying anything," I say quietly to April.

"I get it," April whispers, "but Stephanie is her sister. You're like my sister, and I wouldn't rat you out if you had an affair. Even if she told you as soon as she found out, would it have changed anything? You guys were splitting up anyway, the affair was still a threat to Adam's career, and you both still would have wanted those text messages and photos kept private. I don't think it would have made a difference."

"You're right," I say, "but it still sucks that I feel like I can't trust her and that she's such a good liar."

I sit up and move my large, cinnamon-coloured tote from the chair between April and me to the chair on my other side. As Kelly walks over, I pat the empty chair, motioning for her to sit down.

Kelly sits, puts her drink on the table, her purse on the floor and sighs. I smile at her. Convincing liar or not, if she didn't kill Paul, she's going through a horrible time right now, and needs all the support she can get.

I notice she looks tired and is wearing less makeup

than she usually wears. Her hair is pulled into a low ponytail instead of fully blown out and styled like it usually is when she's working, and the only jewelry she's wearing is her wedding ring and a pair of lovely, delicate, gold love-knot earrings.

"Those earrings are lovely," April says, as if she were reading my mind.

April is good at small talk, a quality I both admire and am grateful for because her gift has saved me from more than one awkward silence.

"Thank you. They were a gift from my grandparents when I was a teenager. They gave us each an identical pair"—Kelly gestures toward the counter where Stephanie is paying for a drink—"but she has a metal allergy and can't wear any jewelry at all, no gold, no silver, nothing. She breaks out in a horrible rash that lasts for days if she even touches the stuff."

Trying not to show a reaction to seeing Stephanie, I move my tote bag from the chair beside me to the floor to make room for her.

"Listen, thanks for coming to Paul's celebration of life yesterday," Kelly says, putting one hand on my lap and her other hand on April's lap. "I wish I could've spent more time with you, but it was busy, and overwhelming. I wanted to talk to everyone and thank each person for coming, but I'm not sure I even had a chance to talk to everyone once."

April puts her hand over Kelly's hand on her knee. "How was your first night back in your apartment?"

"Not good." Kelly shakes her head. "It was harder than I expected."

She perks up. "Stephanie! Over here!" she says, waving until Stephanie sees her and waves back.

I give April a look that I hope says, *Really? We're going to have coffee with Stephanie and pretend we're all friends?*

April gives me a look in return that I interpret as, *I know, just grin and bear it for Kelly.*

"I thought it would be comforting to be back in our apartment," Kelly explains," with all our stuff and happy memories. But I was an emotional mess and ended up calling Stephanie to come and stay with me."

"That's understandable," I say. "It's only been a week, you're still in shock, and maybe until the m—person is arrested, it's safer to not be alone, anyway."

"Look Megan, before Stephanie comes over here…" All three of us glance quickly toward the counter and see that she's still waiting for her coffee. "I'm really sorry I didn't tell you about her and Adam. I honestly didn't know until after Paul died. I found out she was seeing someone the day before he died, but she didn't tell me who it was. That all came out after."

Kelly's version of events matches what Fred told me outside the pub yesterday.

"But, even if I did know, she's my sister, and I don't think I would have been able to tell you. I hated knowing, and I hope this doesn't mean we can't be friends."

Kelly places her hand on my knee again and looks sincere.

"Did you know they used the photos to blackmail

Adam into leaving the firm? So, Stephanie could stay there without Fred having to worry about her and Adam working together?" I ask.

I don't get a chance to gauge Kelly's reaction because Stephanie, drink in hand, is on her way over to the table.

"Hi ladies," Stephanie mutters without looking up from her drink.

"Hi," April and I say weakly in unison.

To distract myself from Stephanie's presence, and wondering what in the heck Adam saw in her, I pick up my cowl and resume knitting.

"Is the salon open again?" April asks while fussing with her bangs.

"Yes," Kelly replies. "The stylists need to get back to work. They worry that their clients might go elsewhere if we're closed for too long, and it's good for me to keep busy."

"She's working at the salon during the day," Stephanie adds, "and after work she comes out to our place in Harmony Hills. She knows there's always a room for her at our house."

Stephanie smiles at her sister.

"It's amazing how well I sleep at Stephanie and Fred's house," Kelly looks wistful. "Almost every night, within an hour of eating supper, I get so relaxed and drowsy that I take myself off to bed, and the next thing I know, it's morning. Stephanie and our mom think it's all the crying and emotions. Grief is exhausting."

"You two are lucky to have each other," I say. "So, how's Fred doing?"

I don't care how Fred is but want to do my part in keeping up this awkward, painful conversation. I take a sip of my iced coffee.

"He's been so great!" Kelly says. "He's upstairs right now grabbing a few things for me to take back to Harmony Hills. I can't handle being in the apartment today, so Fred and Stephanie are making sure I don't have to."

"I think he's packing the car, then we can go." Stephanie looks behind her, "He said he'd pop in to let us know when everything's packed, and we can head out."

April is fussing with her bangs again. "No pressure, Kelly, but when you have time, I'd love to pop into the salon to get my bangs trimmed and maybe have my ends cleaned up. There's no rush, I'm not going to go anywhere else, just let me know when you're ready."

"I think I can squeeze you in tomorrow, hun! Let's pop next door quickly, so I can look at my schedule." Kelly gets up, grabs her drink, and motions for April to follow her.

Next thing I know, they're both gone and I'm alone with Stephanie, pretending this isn't horribly uncomfortable.

"Well, this is awkward," Stephanie says, stating the painfully obvious.

"What, having coffee with my husband's girlfriend?" I shrug. "Just another Thursday, Stephanie."

My tone is sarcastic, and I don't care. I take a sip of my iced coffee, and resume knitting while sending telepathic messages to April to hurry the heck up.

Stephanie clears her throat. "I'm not his g—"

"Girlfriend?" I finish her sentence for her. "You're both on the same page about that. Neither of you want you to be referred to as *Adam's girlfriend*."

I smile and look around to see if there's another free table where I can relocate, alone. Nothing. The unveiling of Latte Da's fall menu is a big event in Harmony Lake and all the tables are full of people enjoying their beverages and the company of friends and neighbours. Except our table. There's no enjoyment at our table. Please come back, April.

"Megan, I'm sorry. It was never my intention to interfere with your marriage. I regret the affair, and I wish it had never happened."

She might think she sounds sincere, but she sounds fake and patronizing.

"So, the affair wasn't part of your blackmail scheme from the very beginning?" I ask.

It's crossed my mind more than once that blackmailing Adam could have been the goal all along. With Adam gone, there's an opportunity for everyone below him to move up a rung on the career ladder, including Stephanie.

"No," Stephanie says emphatically, shaking her head, "there was no scheme. It was a mistake. Adam is charming and handsome, and I was weak."

Sneaky, sneaky Stephanie. I see what you did there. Subtly labeling Adam as the pursuer and minimizing her own role in this mess. I'm starting to think Stephanie is a skilled manipulator and her meek, shy persona is an act.

"I didn't want to blackmail him, or you, that was all

Fred." She looks down at her drink. "But I didn't stop him."

I'm not a lawyer, but I know enough about the law to know that Stephanie just admitted to aiding and abetting a crime. Blackmail is a crime, and Stephanie, aware that it was happening, didn't stop it or interfere. She's a lawyer for goodness' sake, an officer of the court. We both know if I say anything, it would be her word against mine, so nothing will ever come from her admission to me.

"Adam is a senior partner. He has a well-established career and reputation. It would be much easier for him to find a new position than it would be for me as a newer lawyer and junior associate. I love Fred and I want us to get past this, but Fred couldn't get past it as long as Adam and I were working in the same office. I truly am sorry for everything, and I hope your marriage survives this as well."

Stephanie gives me a meek little smile and looks down at her cup. I put my knitting on my lap and lean in toward her.

"I'm telling you this for one reason," I say quietly, holding up my right index finger, "because I don't want you to think anything you or your blackmailing husband ever say or do could have any influence on my life, ever."

I narrow my eyes and look directly into her eyes.

"Adam and I separated months before you two started swapping dirty text messages and photos. You did not destroy our marriage. You aren't significant enough to do that. Your six-week affair didn't end our twenty-year marriage, years of apathy and disinterest did. You came along afterwards, and, knowing Adam as well as I do, you were just a distraction."

I grab my tote bag, drop my knitting inside it, stand up, throw my bag over my shoulder, pick up my coffee, and stride to the door without looking back.

CHAPTER 24

I squint into the sunlight outside Latte Da, slide my sunglasses from the top of my head down to my eyes, and get my bearings.

I walk over to the recycling bin, dump my empty coffee cup inside, and keep walking. I'm making a mental note to text April to explain why I bolted from Latte Da when my left shoulder bumps into the right side of someone walking toward me. I look up to apologize and realize the person I've bumped into is Fred Murphy.

There might only be two of them, but it feels like there's a Murphy everywhere I go today. I nod at Fred and continue on my way, picking up the pace as I walk, putting as much distance between me and the Murphys as this small town will allow.

I turn into the alleyway beside Knitorious, continuing toward my car, and hear my phone ding inside my bag.

I get into my car and lock the door because, on top of everything else that's happened this week, I've become someone who locks her car and house when she's in them to feel safe.

I plug my phone into the console and check my texts; it's Adam. We were just talking about him, his ears must be burning, as my mother used to say when someone she was thinking or talking about would suddenly call or show up.

Adam: *Where are you? Everything OK?*

I start the car and look at the time on the dashboard 1:05 p.m. Shoot, I'm late.

Me: *On my way. Be there in 10.*

While I drive, I think about how the Stephanie I met yesterday at the pub and the Stephanie I spoke with today at Latte Da are like different people. What you see is not what you get with her.

Since first finding out about their affair, I've wondered which one of them made the first move. Fred said it was Stephanie who made the first move, but after meeting meek and mousey yesterday-Stephanie, I couldn't imagine her making a first move to get anything, and figured Adam was more likely the pursuer. But after talking to today-Stephanie, I'm starting to think there's a third possibility: She chased him until he caught her. She let him believe the relationship was his idea, but she was in charge the entire time.

I'm also not convinced Stephanie really sent Fred the photo of Adam by accident. I wouldn't put it past her to send it to him accidentally-on-purpose to expose the affair and eliminate Adam as an obstacle on her career path.

I pull up to 845 Mountain Road and park on the road in

front of a large, Victorian-era house. I sit in the car for a moment and assess my surroundings. Mountain Road is in one of the oldest areas of Harmony Lake. The stately houses are set far back on large lots with mature, leafy trees and tall, imposing coniferous trees that I would guess are even older than the houses.

Several houses have signs indicating they've been converted to duplexes, triplexes, or small professional buildings. The neighbourhood predates sidewalks, and the east side of the road is lined with the old-fashioned lamp posts connected to each other with electrical wires. During tourist season, Mountain Road is well travelled because it's one of the two roads that lead into the mountains and to the two vacation resorts that are busy with skiers in the winter, and escapees from the city in the summer.

I text Adam to let him know I'm outside, get out of the car and lock the door, then listen for the chirp that confirms it's locked and walk up the driveway to the front door.

As I approach the wraparound porch, the large front door opens with Adam on the other side, waving. I can tell he's excited. He's grinning and giddy as he beckons me inside. I haven't seen him this excited about something since he made senior partner at the firm.

Stepping into the foyer, I can tell this isn't one of the houses that's been renovated into residential apartments. It's been renovated into office suites. I try to hide my disappointment and not ruin Adam's obvious joy. Hopefully, he's so wrapped up in his own excitement, he doesn't notice my initial shock that he isn't showing me his new home.

What was likely once a grand foyer is now a waiting room and reception area. There is a sitting area to the right of the stairs with a leather sofa, two leather chairs, a coffee table, and two end tables covered with a variety of magazines and brochures.

To the left is an ornately carved, wooden reception desk and coat rack that look as though they were hand carved specifically to match the restored ornate woodwork of the railings, banisters, and moldings throughout the house.

Behind the wooden desk sits a woman a bit younger than me and wearing a hands-free headset that's almost camouflaged by her black hair. Adam introduces us. Her name is Lin Chow. She's friendly and she has kind eyes.

Lin offers me a selection of refreshments, which I decline. Then Adam takes me on a tour of the main floor, which is mostly meeting rooms, a kitchen, two washrooms, and a supply room with printers, a fax machine, boxes of paper, shredders, and office supplies.

We climb the wooden staircase, and at the end of the hall, on the right, we enter Adam's future office. It's already furnished in the same ornately-carved-wooden theme that was prevalent on the main floor. I look around and decide it's a professional, lawyerly, Adam-like office.

Adam tells me his new neighbours are an accountant, an insurance broker, a financial planner, and a psychologist who specializes in relationship and family counseling.

Despite my disappointment that he isn't moving to 845 Mountain Road to live, I do my best to join in Adam's excitement, and decide not to tell him about my interaction with Stephanie because he's happier, and more hopeful than I've seen him in ages.

We FaceTime Hannah to give her a tour, too, and when we hang up, I notice it's almost 2:30 p.m.

"I need to get going. I want to get to the bank before it closes, then stop by the hardware store," I say.

I need to replace my bank card and get another set of keys cut. Since there's no way to know when the police will return my things, I've decided to replace them.

"I'll walk you out," he says as we leave his new office and turn off the light.

I say goodbye to Lin and tell her it was nice to meet her.

"Congratulations on your new office, it's really great," I say on the porch.

"Thanks. I'll see you at home after your errands."

Adam keeps watch from the porch while I walk to my car, lock myself inside, and drive off.

Seeing how concerned Adam is about our safety is making me paranoid that I'm not concerned enough about it. Was the knitting needle a warning that I could be next? I shudder at the thought, and when I arrive at the bank, I decide to pay to park in a metered spot on the visible and well populated street in front of the bank instead of parking for free in the less visible, more secluded parking lot behind the bank. It makes me sad to change my routine because of this situation, but maybe right now, feeling safe is more important than not feeling sad.

CHAPTER 25

Wʜᴇɴ I ɢᴇᴛ ʜᴏᴍᴇ with my new bank card and keys, I'm shocked to see Ryan Wright kneeling on the front porch, apparently changing the lock on the front door.

"Hey, Ryan!" I stop and smile at him. "Whatcha doin'?"

"Hey, Megan." He pauses his work to talk to me. "Adam texted me last night and asked if I could come over today and re-key the house. So, here I am."

He smiles and shrugs.

"Oh, he didn't mention it."

I'm careful not to let the tone of my voice give away how annoyed I am right now. Thanks for talking to me about the new locks, Adam!

"Listen, Ryan, I'm sorry I questioned your alibi, and I'm sorry if I made you feel like I thought you're a murderer. I spoke with your Dad, and I know you didn't have anything to do with Paul's murder," I say, placing my hand gently on his arm. "Also, congratulations on your three-year chip. I'm really proud of you, and I promise your secret is safe with me. I'd never disclose that to anybody."

"I know you won't say anything." Ryan smiles at me. "And I'm not ashamed of being a recovering alcoholic, but my livelihood depends on people being comfortable enough to let me into their homes and businesses and near their families. Some people would think twice if they knew about my past…issues."

"You'll always have work at chez Martel! The three of us are useless at fixing anything, and if it weren't for you and Archie, we'd be sitting on boxes of flat-packed furniture waiting to be assembled, surrounded by drippy faucets and broken appliances," I joke. Sort of.

I walk past Ryan and go into the house. I hear Adam speaking and assume he's on the phone. Once I'm in the kitchen, I see that he isn't on the phone; he's at the kitchen table on his computer.

"Oscar, stop!" he says when he sees me.

"OK, transcription stopped," Oscar responds.

"It's a transcription app," Adam explains. "Instead of typing a letter, or email, or whatever, I dictate it to the app and a summary is automatically emailed to me. Then I can forward it to whomever I hire as a legal secretary to clean it up and format it for me."

"That sounds cool," I reply. "It could be a real time-saver."

I'm still annoyed about Adam having the locks changed and not talking to me about it first.

"Why is Ryan changing the locks?" I ask, trying to sound non-confrontational.

"Because yesterday a killer had access to your purse and everything in it, including the keys to the house," Adam explains.

And the keys to Knitorious, I realize. I make a mental note to ask Ryan to re-key Knitorious.

"I wish you'd talked to me about it first, since I live here too. In fact, I'm supposed to be the only one of us who lives here. We had a plan, Adam, and you were supposed to find somewhere to live this month, not find new office space. Have you even started looking for an apartment?"

I look at him, waiting for a response.

"I'm not moving out until whoever killed Paul has been arrested," he replies.

"What if no one is ever arrested? What if this turns into one of those cold cases?"

I can hear the frustration in my voice.

"Meg, I'm not budging on this. We might not be together anymore, but right now you're still my wife, and you'll always be Hannah's mother, and we'll always be family. I'm not moving out so you can live alone while a killer roams around town, rummaging around in your purse whenever they feel like it. If you want to deny the seriousness of the situation, that's fine, but you and your denial should get used to having me as a roommate until this murder is solved and the killer is behind bars."

I'm seething. He's decided all of this without talking to

me about any of it, and on top of everything else, he's using his condescending lawyer voice.

"Again, *Adam*." I emphasize his name in the most condescending tone of voice I can, so he knows how it feels. "I'm an adult person who has a right to make her own decisions and have a say in whether our locks are changed and whether you and I continue to live together under the same roof. Maybe *I* should move out and *you* should stay here."

It's an empty threat. I'd never leave my home. It's more my home than his, and we both know that. I chose every piece of furniture, tchotchke, and paint colour. I clean it, maintain it inside and out, and have spent countless nights and weekends alone inside it, raising Hannah, while Adam was elsewhere, focusing on his career.

"Don't be so dramatic, Meg!"

He did *not* just call me dramatic!

"This house is big enough for both of us to co-exist a little while longer without getting in each other's way," he adds.

"You're dismissing my feelings, Adam! Stop doing that!"

"OK, transcription stopped," Oscar says, interrupting my tirade.

We both turn and look at the small device on the end table. Oscar's light changes colour from yellow to blue, and Adam and I look at each other.

"He recorded our argument?" I ask, pointing at Oscar, "And emailed it to you?" I ask, pointing at Adam's laptop.

"Maybe," Adam says, swiping his fingers across the trackpad on his laptop to wake it up.

Staring intently at the screen, he starts typing on the keyboard.

"Sure did! I just got an email of our conversation starting with me saying, 'I'm not moving out until whoever killed Paul has been arrested.' Something one of us said before that must've triggered Oscar to start the dictation app."

I try to think back to what we said that might have triggered Oscar, but it's a jumble of raised voices and hurt feelings. Oscar probably said something like, "Dictation started," but we didn't hear it over our shouting back and forth.

As if I need another reason to solve this murder, Adam's determination not to move out until the killer is behind bars just rocketed to the top of the list.

"That's creepy. Have you ever received emails of our conversations before?" I ask him.

"No," he answers without looking away from his laptop screen, "but I only installed the app a few days ago. I should probably delete it."

We hear a knock at the door.

"Ryan," we say simultaneously.

"I totally forgot he was here," I say on my way to answer it.

"Sorry to interrupt," Ryan says, moving his head from side-to-side in an attempt to look past me into the house, probably to see what all the shouting is about. "Here are your keys."

He dangles two keys, and two business cards between his right thumb and forefinger.

I open my hand and Ryan drops the keys and cards into it. I look at the business cards that have a seven-digit code on the back. Ryan must see my confusion, because he explains that Adam upgraded to smart locks that can be locked and unlocked with either a key, a phone app, or by asking Oscar to lock or unlock the doors.

"Do you want a demonstration?" he asks.

I know I'm not interested in downloading another app, so I decline the demonstration and silently resolve to continue locking and unlocking the doors the old-school way, with a key.

I ask Ryan if he's available to come by Knitorious and change the locks since my keys to Knitorious were also on my missing key ring. He tells me he's leaving tonight for a job out of town and won't be back until Monday night. He says he'll get his dad to put an extra lock on the inside of the front and back doors at the store tonight, to be safe, and he'll meet me at the store first thing Tuesday morning to re-key both doors properly.

Ryan leaves and I give one of the business cards with the code on it to Adam, but don't give him the key. He won't be living here much longer anyway, I reason, so he can use the app.

I open the back door and lift the mat on the back deck. I retrieve the spare key we keep hidden there and replace it with one of the new keys Ryan gave me. When I come back inside, Adam is looking at me.

"You know you'd never use it anyway," I say to him. "You love technology and you'll only ever use the app."

He flips the business card over and uses his cell phone to scan the code on the front, so he can download the app and set it up on his phone.

"Did you know the app works from anywhere in the world? And we can set it so the door locks automatically thirty seconds after it closes?" he asks, super excited about his new tech toy.

I text Hannah to tell her I misplaced my keys and give her the new door code and app info.

CHAPTER 26

Friday, September 20th

When I get to work on Friday, I'm happy to see that Archie has installed a sturdy barrel-lock on the inside of both the front and back doors at the store, just like Ryan said he would.

Connie invites me for a sleepover after work and I accept. Connie and I haven't had a sleepover in months, and I'm grateful for a day off from seeing Adam.

We have a yummy spaghetti Bolognese dinner, apply face masks that promise we will look and feel ten years younger, eat too many chocolate covered almonds, drink wine, and binge-watch the first season of a show about three suburban housewives who hold up a grocery store at gunpoint to solve their financial problems and end up working with an international money laundering ring. Hijinks and hilarity ensue.

Laying in Connie's spare room with Harlow purring

next to my head, I'm more comfortable and relaxed than I have been in days and welcome a good night's sleep.

SATURDAY, September 21st

The store is busy so the day passes quickly. Life is beginning to return to normal in Harmony Lake. The crime scene tape is gone, the salon is open for business as usual, and while people are still talking about Paul's murder and theorizing about who did it and why (the latest theory is he ticketed a mob boss for littering and his death might have been a professional hit), people are also talking about other things, and Paul's murder is beginning to consume a little less of the town's collective consciousness.

After work Connie and Harlow pack a bag and leave to spend the rest of the weekend at Archie's place until the locks are changed on Tuesday. I head home and spend the evening washing, drying, and folding laundry while watching the first few episodes of the second season of the show Connie and I watched last night.

SUNDAY, September 22nd

Adam and I have our weekly FaceTime call with Hannah and hear all about university life and life in the big city. We are relieved and happy to see how well she's adjusting to being away from home. She's definitely adjusting better than we are, but then she's not embroiled in a police investigation.

I spend some time cleaning up the yard, then have a shower and go to April and Tamara's house for lunch.

April makes a delicious cheddar pancetta quiche with thyme and Tamara spoils us with homemade chocolate eclairs. They have a knack for making even the most elegant food look easy to prepare. I tell April about the girl's night Connie and I had on Friday and recommend the show we streamed. While we're talking, both April and Tamara's phones chime.

"It's the WSBA group chat," Tamara says.

"Fred Murphy, Kelly Sinclair's brother-in-law, has been reported missing," April reads. "Anyone with information is asked to contact the police. Then it has Eric's number."

"Isn't that interesting," I say.

"I bet he's done a runner. He did it, and he knows the police are about to arrest him, so he took off." April shrugs her right shoulder.

She's been convinced Fred is the killer since we found out at the pub that he is Paul and Kelly's brother-in-law.

"If he did do it, and now he's on the run, hopefully, he's far away from here," Tamara observes. "Someone that desperate might do anything to avoid being caught. If he's already killed once, he has nothing to lose. Let's hope none of us run into him."

"Let's hope," I say.

"I wonder how long he's been missing. I saw him on Thursday, after my dramatic exit from Latte Da and from Stephanie. He was on the sidewalk outside."

"I didn't see him on Thursday, but I remember Kelly and Stephanie telling us he was loading the car with stuff from Kelly's apartment. They were waiting for him to finish up so they could leave, remember?" April asks, nudging me, and I nod.

"Well, I haven't seen him since I shook his hand at the pub on Wednesday in the condolence line," Tamara adds.

"What if he's not on the run?" I ask. "What if he found out who the real killer is and now, he's dead?"

Ever since the knitting needle from the murder scene turned up in my tote bag, I've been afraid it was a message from the killer warning me not to get any closer or ask more questions.

April and Tamara give me leftovers for Adam, and I successfully resist the urge to eat his eclair on the drive home.

When I walk in the house, Adam is in the family room watching golf on TV.

"April and T sent leftovers for you," I announce, holding up the glass containers with the quiche and eclair inside, "Do you want them now or should I put them in the fridge?"

He pauses the TV, gets up, and comes into the kitchen. He opens the cutlery drawer, grabs a fork, closes the drawer with his hip, takes the rubber lid off the glass container with the quiche, and starts eating while leaning against the counter.

"This is fantastic," he says, using his fork to point at the food in the container.

"I know, right?" I answer. "Did you hear that Fred Murphy is missing?"

I throw it out there without any warning.

"No." He shakes his head and stabs at a piece of quiche without looking up at me.

"Where did you hear that?"

"The girls got a message in the WSBA group chat during lunch. It includes Eric's number and asks for anyone with information to call him."

Adam has the last forkful of quiche and puts the container and his fork in the sink, even though the dishwasher is literally right there, next to the sink. He reaches for the container with the eclair in it.

"The last time I saw Fred was on Thursday when I left Latte Da, right before I met up with you at your office. When did you last see him?"

He turns his back to me, to eat the eclair over the sink.

"Wednesday. At the pub. With you," he says.

We stand in silence for a moment. He finishes his eclair, wipes his hands, and turns to me.

"That was really good. I'm going to text the girls and thank them."

He walks back to the family room, resumes his seat on the sofa, unpauses the TV, and picks up his phone.

CHAPTER 27

TUESDAY, September 24th

Shortly after I open the store, Ryan arrives and gets to work changing the locks. Then a yarn order arrives and I start to unpack it at the Harvest table while he works on the front door, causing the bell above to jingle randomly.

"Thanks for getting here so quickly, Ryan. I know you just got back from working out of town all weekend. I really appreciate it."

"Anything for family!" he replies.

I look at him confused.

"We're practically family now. I mean, Archie's my dad and Connie may as well be your mom, so that kind of makes us...step siblings? I think?"

It's his turn to look confused, but he's right.

"So, when does Adam officially open for business at his new office on Mountain Road?" he asks.

I'm shocked by the question. I didn't realize Adam told anyone about his new practice yet. I've only mentioned it to April and Connie. Maybe Connie told Archie, and Archie told Ryan?

"Sometime next month, I think. I didn't realize he mentioned it to you," I respond.

"He didn't. Lin told me. I think he'll like working there. The building is well-maintained, and Dad and I do most of the maintenance, so you know it's quality work."

"Did Lin mention it when you were there doing a job?" I ask.

"No, she told me at dinner last night," He looks up at me. "We're dating. We had dinner last night when I got back into town."

Another secret I've learned this week. I'll have to remember to add it to the ever-growing list.

"The dating thing with Lin and me is kind of new. Not very many people know yet."

"Well, I hope it works out, if that's what you both want, and you're happy together."

"Thanks, Megan. I have to run to my truck for a few minutes. I'll be back."

Ryan hurries through the store and exits through the back door to the parking lot.

Seconds later, I hear the jingle above the door. Eric enters the store and closes the door behind him.

"Long time no see," I say walking toward him. "Is this a business call or are you taking me up on my offer to teach you how to knit?"

I'm certain it's the former and not the latter, but I'm trying to lighten the mood. He looks serious. His jaw is clenching and the muscles around his eyes are tense.

"We found Fred Murphy," he says.

That's a relief.

"Alive?" I ask.

"He was in the back of a rented cube van parked in front of 845 Mountain Road."

Adam's new office! The look on my face must have betrayed my shock because Eric asks if I'm familiar with that address. I sit on one of the chairs in the cozy area.

"Adam rented an office there. Last week. He's not open for business yet, but he showed me around on Thursday."

"Who else knows he rented an office there, and specifically, who knows you were there on Thursday?"

He pulls his notebook and pen from his breast pocket.

"Hannah, we FaceTimed with her while we were there. Lin, the receptionist. Connie and April. That's it as far as I know. I'm not sure if Adam has told anyone."

Then I remember!

"Oh! And Ryan Wright. He said Lin told him, apparently they're dating."

I don't know how to ask delicately, but I need to know.

"Is Fred OK? I mean was he alive in the back of the cube van?"

Eric shakes his head and the sense of relief I felt disappears.

I sit in shock, twirling my ring while Eric writes in his notebook. The sound of the back-door closing breaks the silence.

"Hey, Detective Sloane," Ryan greets Eric and gets back to work on the front door.

"Hello, Mr. Wright, how are you?" Eric responds.

I think I should make myself scarce, so Eric and Ryan can talk privately.

"I'm just slipping out for a minute to pick up a snack."

I flip the sign on the door from OPEN to CLOSED so they won't be interrupted while I'm gone. "Would either of you like anything?"

They both decline my offer. I leave through the front door and speed walk to Artsy Tartsy.

April is behind the counter serving a customer. I glare at her with my eyes as wide as I can open them. April widens her eyes to match mine and calls to Tamara who comes out of the office, closes the door behind her, and joins April behind the counter. April finishes cashing out her customer, and we all watch as he leaves.

Even though the bakery is empty, I stand on my tippy toes and lean over the counter as far as I can. April and Tamara both lean toward me until our faces are only inches apart.

"They found Fred. He's dead. He was at Adam's new office. In the back of a rented cube van," I say, barely above a whisper.

I tell them I only have a few minutes because I lied about going to get a snack, so I could fill them in and leave Eric and Ryan alone in the store to talk.

With no time to waste, we start brainstorming. Who killed Fred? How did he die? Why did the killer choose that address? To implicate Adam or me? Maybe he killed himself? Maybe he couldn't live with what he'd done? Maybe he found out who the real killer was and was murdered, so he couldn't expose them? Fred was our number one suspect, and now it feels like we're back at square one.

"Maybe there are two killers," April suggests. "Maybe Fred killed Paul, and Fred's murder is revenge."

Her commitment to believing Fred murdered Paul is strong.

"Paul didn't have a lot of friends. Off the top of my head, I can't think of anyone who would kill to avenge his death," Tamara points out.

"But he has a grieving widow," I say.

I tell April and Tamara that Ryan knows about Adam's new office because of his relationship with Lin, and that he was away all weekend working.

"Ryan's alibis aren't always rock solid," April reminds me.

"He's dating Lin, though, and seems to like her, so why would he leave a dead body outside her office?" I check the time on my phone. "I have to get back."

"These will make your snack mission look real," Tamara says, handing me a bag of oatmeal chocolate chip cookies.

I speed walk back toward Knitorious, stop two stores away from the shop, and pull my phone out of my pocket. With the bag of cookies in one hand, I use my free hand to text Adam.

Me: *They found Fred at your new office. He's dead.*

Eric looks up when he hears the jingle above the door. He closes his notebook and clicks his pen closed. I see Ryan working at the back door, and it looks like he's just finishing up. I turn the sign from CLOSED to OPEN and offer Eric a cookie. He declines. Freak. Who says no to a freshly baked oatmeal chocolate chip cookie?

Ryan comes into the store and hands me the new keys and an invoice. I offer him a cookie, and he happily takes one. He says goodbye to Eric and me, picks up his toolbox, and leaves through the back door. I follow him as he leaves and lock the door behind him, being sure to also lock the barrel-lock. Just in case.

I get the feeling Eric is waiting to get me alone so he can ask me more questions.

"Where were you on Friday night, Megan?"

I knew it.

I tell him about my girl's night with Connie and recommend the show we watched.

Does his question mean that Fred's been dead since Friday night? Or is that the last time anyone saw him? Today is Tuesday. We found out Fred was missing on Sunday, so what's the significance of Friday night?

"Where was Adam while you were having a girl's night?"

"I don't know. You'd have to ask Adam." I shrug. "I told you, we don't really monitor each other's whereabouts anymore."

Where were you Adam? All I can think about is his lack of reaction when I told him Fred was missing.

"Why is Friday night important?" I ask him.

"The coroner estimates Mr. Murphy's time of death to be sometime between Friday night and Saturday morning. Hopefully he'll narrow it down even more when he conducts the autopsy today."

That was way more of a response than I was expecting. Or that I'm used to from Eric. Let's see if he keeps it up.

"Did you find him today?" I ask, hoping he's still feeling talkative.

"Last night, a local resident reported a suspicious abandoned cube van on Mountain Road. The caller reported first noticing it early Saturday morning."

That doesn't exactly answer my question, but it's still more information than I expected. I'm surprised news of another crime scene hasn't made its way all over town, and to the WSBA group chat by now. But Mountain Road is mostly commercial, so if this went down last night, after business hours, people might have already left their offices for the day.

Eric thanks me for my time. I offer him another cookie, which he declines because his willpower is obviously superhuman. We say goodbye, and he leaves through the front door.

Adam hasn't responded to my text. I check again, and it says, Read, so I know he's seen it. Where are you Adam? And more importantly, where were you on Friday night?

CHAPTER 28

IT'S ALMOST lunchtime when I hear a knock at the back door of the shop. It's Connie. She has an overnight bag in one hand, and Harlow's kitty carrier in the other. I hold the door for her and notice a box on the ground outside the back door.

"That must be a delivery," Connie observes. "I wish they'd use the front door when no one answers the back one. If there's anyone else in the store, it's almost impossible to hear a knock at the back door. Maybe we should put up a sign."

I pick up the box and carry it to the counter in the store. It's heavier than I expect. Our deliveries are usually yarn so even large boxes don't weigh very much. Connie lets Harlow out of his case and puts her overnight bag on the apartment stairs.

"Funny delivery," I comment to Connie. "There's no shipping label on the box. No return address. Nothing. Are we expecting anything from a local dyer? Maybe it was dropped off."

She shakes her head.

The box is taped shut, and KNITORIOUS is scrawled across the top in black marker. I grab the letter opener from the cup of pens beside the cash register and slice the tape open.

Inside the box is a rock. A familiar rock. I've seen this rock somewhere before. Connie peeks inside the box, but neither of us pick up the grey, heart-shaped rock. Harlow is rubbing his head against the open flaps of the box and tries to jump inside with the rock. Connie picks him up and cuddles him. He purrs but keeps pulling away from her and toward the box, so Connie takes him into the kitchenette and gives him some kitty treats to distract him.

"Why would someone send us a rock?" she asks.

We're both a bit shaken by the weird delivery. This rock is familiar. Where have I seen it before? It's on the tip of my brain, but I can't quite place it. I move the box to the coffee table in the sitting area, where we both sit on the sofa, and resume staring at it.

Connie asks me if I've heard about Fred—and that's when it comes to me!

"This is the rock Kelly uses to keep the back door open at Hairway to Heaven!" I shout, like I'm shouting the winning answer on a TV game show.

Connie and I look more closely at the rock without touching it. It's grey with a few streaks of darker grey, and on one edge, there are rust-coloured blotches.

"Connie, I think this could be blood. I don't remember these blotches when I saw this rock the night Paul died."

Connie walks to the front door, turns the OPEN sign to CLOSED, locks the door, picks up her phone, and calls Eric. I take out my phone and snap a few photos of the rock and the box.

ERIC LOOKS at the rock and nods. This somehow makes sense to him.

"This is another murder weapon, isn't it?" I ask. "Was Fred murdered by chance? Maybe by a hit to the head?"

He doesn't answer me. Instead, he starts asking questions.

He asks what time we noticed the box. I told him what time I opened the door for Connie. Before that, the last person to use that door was Ryan, when he left about two hours before.

No, Connie says, she didn't see any people or vehicles behind the store when she returned.

No, I didn't hear anything strange from the parking lot, and no one knocked at the door, that I heard.

No, the store doesn't have surveillance video.

No, we don't think Wilde Flowers has surveillance video either. In fact, we don't think any of the businesses on Water Street have surveillance video. Well, maybe Charmed & Dangerous, the jeweler, but they're way up the street.

Eric calls for another officer to come and collect the rock and the box it arrived in.

He tells us he's also having the back door dusted for prints, "just in case," then he goes outside and retrieves crime scene tape from the trunk of his car which is parked in front of the store. He uses the tape to block access to the parking lot so cars can't come or go. Then he tapes the area around the back door so no one will touch it or the doorknob.

We watch him go next door to Wilde Flowers. Knitorious shares a driveway and parking lot with Wilde Flowers, so we presume he's going to ask Phillip if he noticed the box, or any people, or cars in the parking lot today.

Standing in the store with Connie and the box, I feel a shiver travel down my spine. Why bring the murder weapon here? Was the killer hoping I'd touch it and leave my fingerprints on it? Is it a warning that I'm next? Is Fred's killer and Paul's killer the same person?

If there are two killers, it's an odd coincidence that they would both send me something from the murder scene. I feel unsafe and can't shake the feeling someone is watching me. It's horrible not knowing who in your small town is killing people and either trying frame you as the murderer or warn you that you're next.

Connie suggests we leave the store closed for the rest of the day. Good idea, though it doesn't seem like we have a choice anyway, since it's basically a crime scene now.

A uniformed officer opens the front door and says he's here to pick up the box and the rock. Out of the corner of my eye, I spy Harlow gracefully and sneakily leap onto the table where the box is. Connie sees it too and scoops him up and away from the table before he can get into the box with the rock. He really wants that box. I offer to take Harlow up to Connie's apartment where he can't cause any trouble.

I take Harlow from her and pick up her overnight bag on my way up the stairs. I put Harlow and the bag in Connie's apartment and close the door before he can bolt back downstairs.

I stop part way down the stairs and text Eric to ask if it's OK to go home. I tell him I feel sick and don't want to be here anymore today.

Then I text April and tell her about the latest murder weapon showing up at Knitorious and text her a couple of the photos. I tell her Knitorious is closed for the rest of the day, and I'm heading home.

Eric texts back and says I can leave. He says he'll drive me. He didn't ask if he could drive me, or if I'd like a drive, he told me he's driving me home. I suspect he wants to speak to Adam before I get a chance to.

I ask Connie if she needs me to stay, and she says no, she'll be fine, and Archie is on his way to keep her company. I tell her the new keys for the store are in the register, along with Ryan's invoice.

Eric and I ride in silence to my house. Adam's car is in the driveway.

I drop my keys on the table by the door and march right over to the dining room table, where Adam is doing whatever it is he does on his laptop.

"Why didn't you respond to my text? I know you saw it!" I say urgently.

I'm almost shouting, not quite, but close.

"Oh, jeez, Meg! I'm sorry," he says, smacking his forehead with his palm. "I did see it, but I was on the phone trying to arrange business insurance for the practice. By the time I hung up, I forgot to text you back."

Really?! I text him that someone is dead, and it slips his mind to text me back?

Eric and I bring Adam up to date, and I show him the photos I took of the rock. He's very quiet, he's thinking.

"You took photos of the evidence?" Eric asks me.

I nod and show him the photos on my phone.

"Other than Connie and April, and now Adam, who else have you shown them to?" he asks.

He's right, but I'm a little offended by his assumption, nonetheless.

"No one else," I say.

"Where were you on Friday night, Adam?" I ask.

I need to know, and Eric would've asked him anyway.

"I was here until about 6 p.m., then I walked over to The Embassy for dinner. Friday is Fish and Chip night, halibut or haddock. I chose halibut. I ate, had a couple of pints, chatted with Sheamus about golf, and left after the Leaf's preseason game ended. I got home around 10 p.m.?"

He snaps his fingers and looks at Eric.

"Phillip saw me, he was pulling into his driveway as I was walking to the front door. We said hello. He wanted to talk to me about the garden."

He looks from Eric to me.

"He says you're an over-waterer, Meg."

I feel guilty thinking even for a minute that Adam might be responsible for what happened to Fred. The Adam I know isn't capable of murder. At least I don't think he is. I hope he isn't.

Is he really incapable of murder, or do I *want to believe* he's incapable of murder? Now I'm second-guessing myself. I feel exhausted, defeated, and confused.

I go into the family room alone and flop onto the sofa. Eric and Adam continue to talk in the dining room, and a few minutes later, Adam walks him to the door and Eric leaves.

"Meg, I think it's time for us to lawyer-up."

"Of course, you do," I respond. "You're a lawyer and lawyers always think that."

I know a lawyer will limit Eric's access to us, and what we can tell him, which would likely slow down the investigation. A lot. I also know that I have nothing to hide because I didn't do anything.

"If you want to lawyer-up, go ahead," I tell him. "I'm not doing anything that might slow down the investigation.

"Speaking of lawyers," he says, "I'm supposed to go on my annual golf retreat tomorrow with the guys from law school, remember? Well, I emailed them and cancelled. I don't feel comfortable being almost four hours away from home with all this going on, and I still have a lot to do if I'm going to be ready to open the practice in three weeks."

What? I completely forgot that was happening this

week. I stopped putting Adam's events in my calendar weeks ago. No! He needs to go. I need him to go. We've been together way too much lately. I would have the house to myself for two glorious nights! This two-night retreat is the break we both need.

"No! Don't do that," I demand, waving both of my hands in front of me. "Email them back and tell them you'll be there. You planned this months ago, and we've already paid for it."

I'm trying to appeal to his sense of practicality.

Think, Megan, think! Give him all the reasons he should go.

"Listen, Adam, you've had a really hard couple of weeks. You left the firm, you've been blackmailed twice, attended a funeral, we've spent an uncomfortable amount of time together which has been stressful, we're being investigated for murder, we're still adjusting to Hannah being away at school, you're trying to set up a new practice in less than thirty days…"

Gosh, it really does sound bad when I say it out loud in one sentence.

"You deserve a couple of days away, to decompress, have some fun, see your buddies, play some golf, and process everything that's been happening."

One last push; I put one hand on my chest and the other on his arm.

"I think it would be unhealthy if you didn't go," I say softly.

"I'll think about it," he says.

CHAPTER 29

W<small>EDNESDAY</small>, September 25th

When I wake up, Adam is loading his golf clubs into his car. I'm relieved he decided to go on his golf retreat.

Before I leave for work, I put a bottle of pinot grigio in the fridge, so it will be chilled when I get home from work. I can't wait to have the house to myself. My big plans include movies, wine, popcorn with extra butter, and finishing Hannah's cowl.

Connie and I work together until lunchtime when she leaves for another mystery appointment, then it's just Harlow and me in the store for the rest of the afternoon.

I package online orders and chat with the local charity knitting guild who come by the store on Wednesdays to knit, discuss future charity knitting projects, and sometimes order yarn for upcoming projects. This month they're working on "knitted knockers" for the Knitted Knockers organization. Knitted Knockers are prosthetic breast inserts that cancer survivors put in their bras after a mastectomy. They're always in demand at local hospitals and cancer support groups. Connie gives the charity guild a discount on the yarn they purchase for charity knitting.

The store usually closes at 6 p.m., but at 5:30 p.m. Harlow and I are the only ones here, so I gather up the online orders I packaged and close early, so I can drop them off at the post office before it closes.

I give Harlow his dinner, hide a few kitty treats in his favourite napping spots, assure him that Connie will be home soon, then lock the door behind me on the way out.

I join the short line at the post office right behind Tamara who's mailing a care package to their daughter, Rachel. Tamara tells me that she and April are going out for dinner and a movie tonight. She invites me to join them, but I decline because I'd rather not be the third wheel on their night out, and I'm looking forward to getting home to my empty house.

Tamara drops off her package, we wish each other a good night when she passes me on her way out, then I drop off the on-line orders and leave.

I drove to work this morning. I need to go back to Knitorious to pick up my car. As I walk past Ho Lee Chow, my tummy rumbles, so I stop and look at the menu in their window and contemplate adding a combo number seven to my evening plans.

I'm perusing the menu when I hear someone call my name.

"Hey Megan! It's nice to see you again. Your curly hair gave you away," a strange man says as he walks toward me.

He's standing next to me now, and he's not at all familiar. I'm sure I've never met him.

"Hi!" I say, "I'm sorry, have we met?"

"You don't remember me? You're breaking my heart, Megan."

He clutches his chest dramatically.

"I was your cab driver the other night," he says, pointing to a taxi parked on the side of the road.

Precious Cargo Cab Company is painted on the side of the car and printed on the roof light. I shake my head. He must have the wrong Megan.

"You flagged me down just off Mountain Road? Really late Friday night...or I guess it was really early Saturday morning. You're even prettier in the daylight, by the way."

I'm still shaking my head, but my interest piques when he mentions Mountain Road and Friday night.

"You said you were at a house party and had a few too many drinks to drive. You were walking home, but when you saw me you flagged me down. You don't remember any of it? You must've had more to drink than I thought."

"Where did you drop me off?" I ask.

"At home. You live above the knitting store, right? I dropped you off out front."

I confirm that he means Knitorious, even though it's the only knitting store in town. He asks again if I live above it, but I don't answer him.

"I was kind of hoping we'd run into each other again," he says. "I was wondering if maybe I could get your number? We got along so well in the cab, but I'm not allowed to ask for a number from a customer. Now that you're not in my cab, you're not technically a customer anymore."

I'm thinking about what he's saying and twirling my ring.

He nods toward my ring. "Is that a wedding ring? I looked for a ring when I drove you home and you weren't wearing one, so I assumed you're single. I'm sorry if I got it wrong."

"Did you happen to notice if I was wearing any other jewelry?" I ask.

"I don't think so." He shakes his head. "Or if you were, I didn't notice. Why? Did you lose something that night? I didn't find any jewelry when I cleaned out the cab after my shift. Sometimes I find an earring or a broken necklace or something, but nothing after my shift on Friday night."

He pauses for a moment.

"Is getting your number out of the question, or what?"

I don't give him my number. Instead I ask him for his number and name, and he happily gives me both. He has to go; he's in a hurry to pick up an order from Ho Lee Chow and deliver it to a customer. He says he hopes to hear from me soon and disappears into the restaurant.

He'll hear from someone soon, that's for sure.

I use my phone to take a couple of photos of his cab, being sure to get both the license plate number and the cab number.

I dial Eric's number and start walking briskly toward my car. He's not answering. Where is he? I text him the photos of the cab, the driver's name and number, and highlights of what the cab driver said about our alleged interaction on Friday night.

I was neither at a house party, nor intoxicated on Friday night or Saturday morning, and I was never in a cab. Unbeknownst to the driver, it wasn't me in the back of his cab on Friday night. It was Fred and Paul's killer.

I walk faster, twirling my ring as I close the distance between me and my car. When I turn into the driveway beside Knitorious, I sprint across the parking lot to my car, and lock myself safely inside.

Now what do I do?

Should I call April? No, this investigation shouldn't upend anyone's life more than it already has, and I don't want to interrupt her and Tamara's night out. Between raising two kids, running a business, and the hectic pace of their lives, date nights are few and far between, and require a lot of planning and scheduling. I'm all too familiar with the consequences of ignoring the required maintenance of your marriage.

Should I call Connie? No, Connie is with Archie tonight, and I'm not convinced she's being completely honest about the mystery appointments she's had lately. I don't want to do anything that would cause her to worry or stress if it might impact her health.

Should I call Adam? What good would that do? He's four hours away from Harmony Lake and it's late in the day, so he's probably finished golfing and had a few drinks with his buddies by now.

Maybe I should call Kelly? No. If I'm right, calling

Kelly could put both of us at risk, so I cross that option off my mental list of potential next moves.

Why hasn't Eric called me back? I decide to drive home, put on my pyjamas, then decide what to do next. Hopefully, in the meantime, I'll hear from Eric.

I plug my phone into the console, so I don't miss his call or text, start the car, and steer it toward home.

At home, I lock the front door behind me and double check that I have my phone and didn't leave it in the car. Phone in hand, I put my tote bag on the bench by the door and head toward the kitchen.

I gasp.

I feel my heart and stomach switch places.

"What are you doing here? How did you get in?"

CHAPTER 30

STEPHANIE MURPHY IS SITTING at my kitchen table. She's facing me, and there's a gun on the table in front of her. Her hair is in a bun, and she's wearing leather gloves. The expression on her face is blank. Her eyes are empty and soulless.

I move the hand that's holding my phone to behind my back.

"Hi Megan. I let myself in using the spare key you keep under the mat at the back door."

She points to the table in front of her. "Put your phone here, please. I know it's in your left hand behind your back."

I move slowly toward the table. Stephanie grips the handle of the gun while, slowly and gently, I put my phone on the table, face up. I take a few steps backwards without taking my eyes off Stephanie and the gun.

"That's far enough," she says.

"How did you know about the spare key under the mat?" I ask.

"You're so predictably suburban, Megan. It was literally the second place I looked," she replies, rolling her eyes and smiling smugly at her own resourcefulness.

"What do you want?" I ask.

"To plant some evidence that will leave no doubt you killed Paul and Fred, then kill you... Or more accurately, help you put yourself out of your misery."

"Adam will be back soon," I lie.

She shakes her head. "Not according to the GPS tracker I have on his car."

Without breaking eye contact with me, she reaches into a pocket, retrieves her phone, and places it on the table in front of her. Then with one hand on the handle of the gun, she uses her teeth to remove the glove from her other hand and unlock her phone.

"He's over three hours away at a golf resort. We both know he won't be back tonight," she says.

She lets go of the gun to put her glove back on, but keeps it close to her, and doesn't let go of it long enough for me to do anything, like run out of the house or snatch the gun away from her. I need to distract her while I think of a way to get out of here. I have to keep her talking.

"Where's Kelly? Won't she wonder where you are?" I ask.

Please don't tell me you've hurt Kelly or that she's in on this with you.

"Don't worry about Kelly. She's sound asleep and won't wake up until tomorrow morning. I'm getting better at dosing the sleeping medication, so she sleeps deeply enough and long enough not to notice I'm gone but doesn't wake up groggy and suspicious."

"You drug your sister?"

"Only sometimes"—she shrugs—"like tonight, so I can visit you, and Friday night when I had to sneak out to...take care of Fred. Other than that, just here and there to help her sleep without waking up in the night to cry over her loser of a husband. What a waste of tears."

She obviously hated Paul.

"I also drugged Fred the night I visited Paul. And tonight, I'm going to drug you, except you won't wake up."

She smiles.

She's a psychopath. I have to figure a way out of this.

"Your phone will give you away. If the police check it, they'll know you were here. If you leave now, I won't say anything. If anyone asks, I'll say you came by to pick something up for Kelly."

I know she won't take me up on it, but I need to prolong this conversation as long as possible while I plan my escape.

"It's a burner and I'll dispose of it as soon as I leave."

Of course, it is.

"Like down a sewer grate or something?"

Ding!

Before she can answer me, my phone dings and we both look at the screen. It's a text.

Eric: Call me.

I take a step forward, and Stephanie shakes her head and points the gun at me.

Brrrrring! Brrrrring! My phone lights up. Now Eric is calling me, and I've never ever wanted to answer a phone call so much in my life.

With one hand still pointing the gun at me, Stephanie reaches out with the other gloved hand and presses the power button until the phone is turned off.

"I kind of understand why you killed Paul. He was using the photos he stole from Kelly to blackmail people and might expose your affair, but why would you kill Fred? He's your husband. He loved you, he told me at Paul's celebration of life."

"You're partially right. I didn't want my affair with Adam to become any more public than absolutely necessary, and Paul stealing the photos from Kelly was the final straw. The real reason he had to go was to save my sister. He was a loser, and he sucked her dry financially over and over again, yet she insisted she loved him, and refused to leave him. He just kept dragging her down with him. He knew she was too good for him, that's why he kept such a close eye on her phone and her email. He was afraid she'd realize she could do better and leave him."

"So, you went to see Paul to kill him?" I clarify.

Using yarn and a knitting needle that just happen to be at the crime scene, before sunset, with his wife right downstairs doesn't seem well planned to me.

"No. I never planned to kill anyone. When Fred found out about Adam and me, we decided there could be no more secrets. We both had to come clean about everything if we were going to stay together and make it work. That's when Fred told me that he loaned Paul money to pay off his latest gambling debt and stop a lien from being placed on the building where they live and where my sister's salon is located."

The tone of her voice is getting angrier as she speaks.

"If they lost that building, she would have lost her home and her business. I was furious. To make it worse, Fred told me about Paul's plan to pay us back by robbing my sister's business and selling her equipment to some buyer he lined up. He said Kelly wouldn't lose any money because the equipment was insured."

She shakes her head, and I think I see tears welling up in her eyes.

"Fred seemed OK with this, which made me more furious. That evening, after I helped Fred fall asleep, I left my phone at home and drove to Harmony Lake. My plan was to tell my sister about Paul's latest gambling debt, Fred's loan to stop the foreclosure of the building, and her husband's plan to steal from her and her business."

Her eyes are definitely watery. She stops for a few breaths. If she wasn't planning to kill anyone, why did she leave her phone at home?

"Would you like a glass of water?" I ask.

Maybe I can throw the glass at her head and run away. She shakes her head.

"When I got to the salon, the back door was propped open with a rock. I went inside, but Kelly was busy with a customer and didn't notice me. I decided to wait upstairs. It never occurred to me that he would be there. He's part of so many clubs, committees, and organizations that Kelly says he's out almost every evening. But when I opened the door, there he was, standing in the kitchen in his undershirt pouring a giant bowl of cereal. I felt sick just looking at him. I confronted him. I told him I knew about the gambling, the near-foreclosure, and the robbery plan. He was smug and arrogant."

My eyes are still locked with Stephanie's, but in my peripheral vision, through the window behind her, I see movement. Like there's a large animal in the bushes. The largest animal we usually get in our backyard is a squirrel. I blink in an attempt to reset my vision in case my eyes are playing tricks on me.

"He held up his phone to show me the photos. He admitted he'd stolen them from Kelly's phone. He told me that if I said anything, he'd make sure the photos and texts would arrive in the inboxes of every lawyer, at every law firm in the country. Then he said he wanted twenty thousand dollars to keep quiet. He gave me until midnight to transfer the money into his account. He told me to leave or he'd start posting the photos to social media sites right then. He turned the TV on and sat at the table to eat his cereal."

She's talking like she's in a trance. There's no more emotion, and her tone of voice is eerily even and calm. She's looking right into my eyes, but I'm not sure if she sees me, or the events she's reliving. She still has one hand on the gun.

"I started to leave, but part way down the stairs, I

decided to threaten to have him charged with extortion and harassment. So, I turned around and went back to the apartment. The TV was blaring. He didn't hear me open the door. He was sitting at the table with his back to me. I could hear him slurping his cereal. I saw an opportunity. There was yarn and knitting needles right in front of me. I grabbed the yarn which was already in a big loop. I wrapped it around my hands and put one of the knitting needles in my mouth. Then I sneaked up behind him, put the loop of yarn around his neck, and tightened it as much as I could. It wasn't tight enough, so I used the knitting needle as a garrote to tighten the yarn more. He tried to pull the yarn away from his neck, and he was kicking his feet, but then he stopped. I let his head fall forward into the bowl of cereal. I thought he was dead, but I wasn't sure. I hoped he was dead. I didn't hang around to make sure. I pulled the needle out of the yarn and left the same way I came in."

She blinks a few times quickly and seems to come back to the here and now. She uses a gloved hand to wipe her eyes.

"When you think about it, I kind of did you and Adam a favour by killing Paul. If he had made those photos public, it would have ruined all of our lives."

I hope she isn't expecting me to thank her.

Stephanie pulls a pill bottle from her jacket pocket and puts it on the table with the gun and my phone.

"I'd really like a glass of wine. Would you like some wine?" I ask.

I don't want wine. I want the bottle to use as a weapon

so I can separate Stephanie from her gun long enough to get away.

"No thank you, but you go ahead. You'll be having some wine soon anyway," she says smiling, and shaking the pill bottle.

Slowly, I walk to the cupboard to get a glass. A broken piece of glass might make a good back-up weapon if my wine bottle idea doesn't work. I swallow hard, nervous about turning my back on Stephanie long enough to retrieve the wine bottle from the fridge.

"Why did you kill Fred? Was it because he found out you killed Paul?"

"No, he was convinced it was either you or Adam."

As she speaks, I open the fridge and get the wine, then turn to face her again.

"After Paul died, we found out he had no insurance. My sister couldn't afford his final expenses, so Fred and I paid for everything. Fred was angry about all the money Paul had cost us, so he decided to follow through with Paul's plan to burglarize the salon. I told him not to because he'd go to jail, but he didn't listen to me. On Friday night, he told me there was a problem at work, and he had to go in for a few hours."

I open the bottle and leave it on the counter to breathe while I choose my moment.

"I had a feeling he was lying and I was right. I have a GPS tracker on his car, too, and it showed him at a location that isn't his work. I went there, and it was a truck rental place. I knew right away what he was up to, so I drove to the salon and found him. He'd just parked the truck by the back door. I tried to reason with him. I begged him not to do it. He told me this was all my fault because of the affair. He said if I hadn't had an affair, then you and Adam wouldn't have killed Paul to keep it a secret, and Paul wouldn't have died before he could pay us back."

Boy did Fred have that wrong. I pour some wine into the glass.

"When he turned away from me to open the rolling door on the back of the truck, I picked up the rock by the salon door and hit him in the head with it. The top of his body fell into the open truck, I just had to lift the bottom half of his body up there, too. After I locked him in the back of the truck, I had to decide what to do next. I'd been watching Adam's GPS, and knew he'd been spending time at 845 Mountain Road, so that's where I decided to leave Fred and the truck. I pointed the evidence back to you and Adam every chance I got. After I dropped off Fred, I even pretended to be you when I hailed a passing cab. It was late, I was too tired to walk back to Water Street. I had the cab driver drop me off outside Knitorious, then I walked back to the salon to get my car and the rock."

Murder must be exhausting. I pick up the wine glass and swirl the contents around in the glass.

"I told the driver my name was Megan. It was dark, we have similar hair, and similar body types, so I figured if the police asked the cab driver who was in his cab, he'd lead them to you." She shrugs one shoulder.

Now or never, I guess. I put the wine glass to my mouth and take a small sip. When I place the glass back on the counter, I intentionally miss and the glass shatters on the wood floor.

"Darn it!" I yell as the wine glass hits the floor. I jump back, away from the shattered glass and splattered wine.

Stephanie grabs the gun and stands up. My plan required her to be so startled that she jumps up without grabbing the gun first. She looks cautiously from me to the mess on the floor, then back to me.

"I better pick these up."

With my eye on the biggest, sharpest shard of glass, I bend down to pick it up.

"Stop!" Stephanie shouts. "Don't move!"

I hear something click and assume she cocked the gun. I put my hands up by my shoulders and slowly stand up.

"OK, transcription stopped," says Oscar's humanoid voice.

I guess Adam hasn't gotten around to uninstalling the dictation app.

Stephanie looks in the direction Oscar's voice came from, then looks back at me.

"Who said that and what does it mean?" She's holding the gun higher. Now, it's aimed at my head.

I tell her about Oscar and explain the dictation app that Adam installed.

"You know Adam and technology," I say, trying to de-escalate her stress level since she's pointing a gun at my head. "He has to try all the new gadgets, he just can't help himself."

I explain that this particular app seems to have a glitch and sometimes starts recording when it's not supposed to.

"How do we erase it?"

I can hear panic in her voice.

"We don't," I tell her. "The transcript is sent to Adam's email. It's probably already in his inbox."

She looks scared, and I hope she's scared enough to make a mistake but not scared enough to shoot me.

"Go get it and bring it here," she demands, waving the gun between me and Oscar.

With my hands still up, I walk slowly to the end table. I can see the front door from here. I could be out of the house in less than three seconds. I squat slowly, turning my head toward Stephanie to tell her I have to lower my hands to move the table and pull the plug out of the wall.

I could simply pull the cord out of the back of Oscar, but I have a new plan.

She nods and as I turn my head away from her and back to Oscar, I see a brief, moving blur out of the corner of my eye, near the front door. I'm convinced the stress of this situation is making my eyes play tricks on me.

I lower my hands and pretend to reach behind the table, but I pick up the heavy ceramic yarn bowl instead. I begin to stand up, my back still to Stephanie, and hold the yarn bowl against my chest like a Frisbee.

I turn quickly and hurl the yarn bowl, as though it were a Frisbee, through the air at Stephanie's head. She instinctively raises her hands to protect her face and points the gun at the ceiling.

I run.

"Oscar! Unlock the door," I shout.

"OK." Oscar replies.

As I turn the doorknob, I'm aware of a shuffling sound behind me and, without looking, assume Stephanie is coming after me. As the door opens, I hear a single gunshot followed by a thud.

Police come rushing through the door I just opened. The first cop shoves me into the corner and stands, gun drawn, with his back to me like a human shield. I crouch down to make myself the smallest target possible and try to peek around and through his legs.

I see a gun on the floor in the family room. My human shield adjusts his stance slightly, and I can see the top half of Stephanie. She's face down and has a knee wedged in her back. Someone is cuffing her hands behind her back. The cop on her back leans forward. It's Eric.

"He's been hit!" a woman's voice yells.

Who was hit? He who? Did Stephanie shoot Eric?

"Who was hit?" I ask my human shield.

He either doesn't hear me or is ignoring me; either way he doesn't answer. I ask louder. Still no answer.

There are police officers all over the house, inside and out, and police lights reflecting on the walls through the windows.

"All clear!" the woman yells.

The human shield moves aside, turns to face me, takes my arm, and helps me up from my crouched position.

"Are you OK?" he asks, looking me over for signs of injury.

I nod.

Physically I'm OK. Other than that, well, I'm not sure yet, stay tuned.

Eric removes his knee from Stephanie's back, stands up, and comes over.

"Were you shot?" I ask, looking for evidence of a gunshot wound.

"No one was shot," he says, smiling.

How can he smile? Smiles in the face of murder, turns down fresh oatmeal chocolate chip cookies, definitely a freak. A freak who just saved my life.

"I heard a gunshot," I insist. "I heard someone say, 'He's been hit.'"

"She was holding up Oscar when she said that," he explains. "Stephanie shot Oscar. He was the only casualty here. Well, Oscar and your yarn bowl."

"Poor Oscar," I say.

I'll miss him.

ERIC GOT the photos I texted to him of the cab and the information about the driver. When I didn't answer his text or phone call, he knew there was a problem, so he came to the house, peered in a few windows, and assessed what was happening. Then he contacted Adam who used the app on his phone to unlock the house. Back-up arrived without lights and sirens, and the officers surrounded the house, carefully positioning themselves so Stephanie wouldn't see them if she looked outside. This explains the movement I saw in the back garden.

Eric sneaked in and hid, biding his time until the gun was pointed away from me and it was safe to intervene.

He was the blur I saw near the front door just before I made my escape attempt. Hurtling the yarn bowl at Stephanie's head gave him the opportunity he needed to sneak up behind her and take her down, and gave me the opportunity to get out of the line of fire. That was the shuffling sound, gunshot, and thud I heard when I opened the door. Eric lunged at her from behind and grabbed both of her wrists, commandeering her arms. With her arm extended, and the gun pointed toward the end table with Oscar on it, the gun discharged, then she went down face first with Eric on her back. Oscar was in the wrong place at the wrong time.

CHAPTER 31

WEDNESDAY, October 2nd

April and I went to Toronto for a few days to visit Hannah and Rachel. We did some shopping, saw a musical, then stopped on our way home for two days of pampering and spa treatments at Ste. Anne's Spa. The break gave me the time and space to process everything that happened last week with Stephanie.

When I got home last night, there were boxes scattered around the kitchen and dining room. Moving boxes. Adam is moving! He's moving into one of the new condos at the Harbourview Condominiums. He gets possession this weekend and plans to move on Saturday, if I'm sure I'm ready to be alone in the house. I am.

Besides, while I was away, he had a state-of-the-art security system installed, complete with cameras, so I probably live in the safest house in Harmony Lake.

I'm off this morning, but I'm working this afternoon. I

decide to walk to work and stop at Latte Da on my way to the store.

I'm standing in line, trying to decide what to order, when Kelly comes in.

"I saw you walk past the salon and took a chance that you would stop for coffee," she says hesitantly.

I throw my arms around her. We hug tightly and both start crying. Ugly crying. Sobbing. The kind of loud, wet, messy crying that can't be done discreetly. We help ourselves to napkins and find a quiet corner where we begin apologizing profusely to each other.

She's sorry for not realizing her sister is a psychopath. I'm sorry she lost so many people. She's sorry she didn't tell me as soon as she realized her sister was having an affair with Adam. I'm sorry I suspected her of murder. She's sorry she hasn't called since Stephanie almost killed me. I'm sorry I didn't call her to warn her as soon as I figured out Stephanie was the killer. When we're out of tears and apologies, we get back in line to order our coffees.

"Eric let me see Stephanie," Kelly says softly while we're waiting for our orders. "I asked her to take responsibility for everything she's done and not cause any more suffering with a trial. She agreed."

"It's over? Like, completely over?" I ask.

"It's over," she assures me.

We get our coffees and go outside. After one more hug, we agree to meet at Ho Lee Chow for dinner tonight after work. She goes back to the salon, and I continue on my way to Knitorious.

The jingle of the bell above the door, and the warm, comforting smell of the store hit me at the same time, and I realize how much I've missed being here. I close the door behind me and stand still for a moment letting the comfort wash over me and through me.

"Welcome back, my dear."

Connie comes over and gives me a long hug.

"This store hasn't been the same without you," she says when she finally lets me go.

Archie stands up and gives me a hug.

"Welcome back, Megan. Thank goodness you're OK."

We sit down in the cozy area, Harlow wakes up from his nap in the front window, has a long stretch, slinks over to us, and graces my lap with his presence. While he purrs, Connie and Archie ask after Hannah and Rachel, so I pull out my phone and show them photos of our visit while Connie fusses over me and strokes my hair.

I tell them that Adam is moving out. They already know. Apparently, I'm the last one to find out.

"It'll be nice to have him as a neighbour," Connie says.

She and Archie exchange a sneaky glance.

"I don't follow," I say.

"Well, my dear, Archie and I also purchased one of the new condos. We've decided it's time to take our relationship to the next level. I was going to move to Archie's house"—she gestures to Archie—"but Ryan lives there, too, and he probably doesn't want to live with two senior citizens."

"And I'd love to move here," Archie adds, "but the stairs to the apartment are too much for my hip."

He sways his hips to illustrate his point.

"So, we decided a new condo would be perfect. It's not his, it's not mine, it's ours."

She's so happy that she's positively glowing.

"And it's perfect for the 'retirement lifestyle' we're trying out," Archie says, using air quotes around "retirement lifestyle."

Wow. A lot can happen in a week.

"I'm happy for you. It's wonderful news. So, is that what all your mystery appointments have been about? You were house hunting?"

"Yes!" Connie taps my knee. "I'm so glad we've decided, and it's over. If I never shop for another house or condo again, that will be fine with me."

"I assume Harlow will move with you to the condo. Or will he be commuting daily?" I ask.

Connie and Archie laugh.

"He's coming with us, but we're planning to do some travelling, and we'd like leave him here at the store while we're away. If that's OK with you, my dear."

Of course, it's OK with me. Harlow belongs here. He's as much a part of Knitorious as Connie and the yarn.

"Who will run Knitorious while you two are travelling and trying out a 'retirement lifestyle?'" I ask, using air quotes for the first time in my life.

"Why, you will of course," she says like it's the most obvious thing in the world. "This store needs you and you need this store. I'm not the only one starting a new phase of my life. You aren't a wife and full-time mother anymore.

You're a soon-to-be-single woman with a grown child and a business to run."

"So, you want me to work here full-time?" I clarify.

"I want you to *own* it, my dear. We'll work out the details later, but trust me, you need this store and this store needs you. I knew when I met you almost seventeen years ago that you would take over this store one day."

For the second time today, I feel myself tearing up. Connie takes my hand and Archie gets the box of tissues from the counter.

"I'll still be here part-time, when we aren't travelling," she explains, waggling her index finger. "You'll never get rid of me completely, no matter how hard you try. But it's time for me to move aside and watch you blossom and make this store your own."

I don't know what to say and I don't think I'm able to say anything through the lump in my throat, so I nod and reach over to hug her, squishing Harlow in the process.

The bell above the door jingles. Connie gets up and greets Eric while I dry my eyes and pull myself together. She and Archie are telling him about their new condo. Why is it, every time I see him, I've either just been crying, or I'm on the verge of crying? He must think I'm an emotionally unstable mess. I stand up and turn around to face them.

"Hi Eric," I say.

He hasn't gotten any less attractive while I was away. On the contrary, he's even hotter than I remember.

"Hi Megan. Welcome home. Don't worry, I'm not here to question you."

I think this is the first time I've heard him have a sense of humour. Solving this case agrees with him, this is the most relaxed I've ever seen him.

"I'm returning the items we took into evidence. The huge purse and its contents," he says handing me a gift bag and a large evidence bag filled with smaller evidence bags. "Except the knitting needle. We have to keep that."

He can keep the knitting needle forever, that's fine with me. I never want to see it again. I put the evidence bag behind the counter and start to open the gift bag.

"It's a small token of my appreciation for all the help you gave me with this case," he says.

It's a new sheep-shaped yarn bowl. To replace the one that broke when I hurled it at Stephanie's head.

"I know it's not the same as the one you made," he explains, "but Connie gave me the number of a local potter who makes yarn bowls, so I could get you a replacement."

"Thank you," I say. "That's so thoughtful. I love it. Actually, I have something for you, too."

I go back to the sofa and reach into my caramel-coloured tote, pull out a gift bag, and hand it to him.

"I was going to drop it off at the station later. It's a small thank you for saving my life, and my reputation, and believing I was innocent."

He opens the bag and pulls out the hat and scarf I knitted for him with yarn I picked up at Romni Wools while April and I were in Toronto. I was able to knit them mostly in the car when it was April's turn to drive, and at the spa. I chose a worsted weight, merino blend in the same shade of forest green as the polo shirt he wore the night we had dinner at the store and he questioned me. The yarn has honey-coloured flecks of tweed that match the honey-coloured flecks in his eyes.

He did save my life; it's the least I could do.

He looks visibly touched by the gift. Or he has good manners and is a good actor. He clears his throat.

"Thank you. I love them. No one has ever knit me anything before."

"Really? Well, I knit a small gift of appreciation for everyone who saves my life, so if you ever save me again, there will be more knitted gifts in your future."

He laughs. "I'll keep that in mind."

"So, what's next for you?" I ask. "I'm sure you're happy to wave goodbye to our quirky little town and watch us fade in your rear-view mirror as you move on to bigger and better cases."

"Funny you ask," he says. "Harmony Lake PD has decided to have their own major crimes unit, and they've offered me a position in the new department."

"And?" I ask. "What did you say?"

"I hope they offered to make you the head of the department," Connie adds.

"I accepted," he answers me, then looks at Connie. "And yes, I will be in charge of the unit. The unit of one. Me. I will be the entire major crimes division."

We all congratulate him, and Archie shakes his hand.

"This town is perfect for me. I can fish in the summer and ski in the winter, and with the low crime rate, I should have enough time off to enjoy both."

I guess I'll be seeing him around town now that he'll be a local.

He asks if we can recommend a real estate agent since he'll need somewhere to live in town. Connie asks him what he's looking for in a home, and he lists his criteria: something small, no yard to maintain, and centrally located. He says he doesn't have very much stuff but needs enough room to store his fishing gear, ski equipment, and a jet ski.

Connie looks at me. I look back at her and smile. She widens her eyes and upgrades her look to a glare, and I'm starting to sense that I'm missing something. She opens her eyes even wider and nods her head. She's obviously trying to tell me something, but I'm not getting it. I'm better at this game when I play it with April.

Connie gives up, lets out an exasperated sigh, and throws her hands in the air.

"It just so happens, Detective Sergeant, that I'll be moving out of the upstairs apartment in the next few weeks, and it will be vacant."

"Would you consider renting it to me? It would be perfect!" Eric says.

"We'll have to ask the owner," she replies, looking at me.

I smile, sure that I'm missing something again.

"Well, Megan, will you be looking for a tenant for the upstairs apartment?" she asks.

It's me! I'm the owner. I forgot. I try to catch up to everyone else in conversation.

"Yes! I'd love to have you upstairs," I declare, feeling

myself start to blush as soon as the last word leaves my mouth.

I'm sure Eric knows what I mean. Talking to him as a cop was easier than talking to him as a...friend? Potential tenant? Neighbour?

Harlow is winding himself around Eric's ankles. Thank you, Harlow, for the distraction.

"Harlow obviously wants you to move in, and I can't say no to him," I say.

"You've never seen the upstairs apartment, have you Eric?" Connie asks. "Megan, why don't you take Eric upstairs, so he can see what he's getting himself into before he commits."

"Sure!" I look at Eric. "Do you have a few minutes now?"

"Lead the way," he says.

As we climb the stairs, Eric says, "I had no idea you own Knitorious. I thought Connie was the owner."

"Ditto," I say.

I open the door to the apartment and we step inside.

"I only found out a few minutes before you got here that I'll be the owner," I explain. "I'm still getting used to the idea. There's been a lot of change in the last few months, you know? Hannah moved away, my marriage ended, I was a murder suspect, then almost a murder victim, and now I'm about to become a business owner. It's a lot to keep up with."

"You'll be an amazing business owner. And landlady."

He walks around and looks at the apartment.

"This place is perfect! I love it!"

"Then it's yours! You can move in as soon as Connie moves out. Listen Eric, I want to thank you again for saving my life. I'm not sure it would've ended well if you hadn't shown up."

"Yes, it would," he says, nodding. "You're smarter and tougher than you give yourself credit for." He winks and I feel a flutter in my belly.

He walks into one of the bedrooms and raises his voice so I can still hear him, "I think you have it backwards, I might have saved Stephanie from you." He comes back into the kitchen. "You would've fought your way out of there, and you would've won. Whether any cops showed up or not, trust me, I have good instincts about these things." He smiles. "And please stop thanking me now."

"Just one more." I hold up my index finger. "Thank you for putting up with me nosing around in your investigation. I'm sure it didn't make your job any easier."

"Actually, you were helpful. You'd make a great partner," he says.

"That was it," I say, "The last thank you. Well for this. If you do something else nice for me, I reserve the right to thank you for it."

"Deal," he agrees, extending his hand, and we shake on it.

"Harmony Lake isn't usually this exciting, you know," I warn him. "If you're expecting a steady flow of murder investigations, you might be disappointed and get bored when you realize the major crimes unit solves cases like littering, jaywalking, and double parking. Maybe you should sign a short-term lease in case you miss the excitement of the big city."

"I have a feeling Harmony Lake is more exciting than it looks, and if it isn't, that's fine with me. I'm ready for a bit of boredom. It'll be a nice change."

We laugh and head back downstairs.

KILLER CABLES

CHAPTER 1

"Who's a smart girl? It's you! That's right, you're a smart girl!" I say with a high-pitched and excited voide.

I squeeze the plush duckie to make it quack and toss it across the room.

"Go get it Sophie!"

Sophie scurries across the wood floor and down the hall. She doesn't apply her corgi-brakes fast enough and slides past the duckie and into the carpet by the front door. She shakes it off, picks up the duckie and prances back to me proudly with her head held high.

Sophie has been staying with me since last week when her human, Laura Pingle, slipped on a patch of ice while taking her trash to the curb and broke her leg in two places. Laura was rushed to the hospital, had to have emergency surgery, and I jumped at the opportunity to look after Sophie until she gets home.

"Which sweater do you want to wear today, Sophie?"

Laura is a knitter, so Sophie has an impressive wardrobe of hand-knit dog sweaters. I grabbed about eight of them when I picked up Sophie's supplies at Laura's house and I left behind at least eight more. Most of them have some shade of purple as either the main colour or an accent colour.

"How about this one?" I ask, holding up her purple and black hounds tooth sweater with a folded turtleneck.

She doesn't disagree (she never does, she's an easy going roommate), soI slip the sweater over her head. By instinct, she lifts one paw, then the other so I can feed them through the impossibly short sleeves of the sweater; she's done this before and knows the drill.

I attach her purple leash to her purple collar, slip on my winter boots, crush my curly, chestnut-brown hair under a hand-knit hat, wrap the matching scarf around my neck, put on my coat, and zip it up.

I check my pockets to make sure my gloves are there, check Sophie's leash to make sure we have enough poop bags for the day and grab my cranberry-coloured tote bag.

One last look in the mirror by the door; I remove a stray eyelash from under one of my hazel eyes, pull my lip balm from my purse and smear a layer on my lips to act as a barrier against the cold, dry, winter air.

"Oscar, I'm leaving," I say into the void.

"OK. I'm arming the house," Oscar replies in a humanoid voice.

Oscar is a digital voice assistant. This is my second Oscar. My ex-husband, Adam, and our eighteen-year-old daughter, Hannah, gave him to me for Christmas.

I call him Oscar 2.0. because Oscar 1.0 died suddenly last September when he was shot by a killer who broke into my house to kill me. Thankfully, Oscar 1.0 was the only fatality that night. The killer's previous two victims weren't as lucky; they lost their lives, I only lost a WI-FI enabled device.

Sophie and I leave the house and I hear the door lock behind me. Good job, Oscar.

I started the car ten minutes ago using the remote starter on my keychain. It's too cold to walk to Water Street, so Sophie and I get in the warm car for the short drive to work.

***

I park in the small parking lot behind the store, and instead of going in through the back door like I would normally, Sophie and I walk around to the front of the store and across the street to the park so Sophie can have a walk and do her business.

This time of year, this early in the day, and this close to the lake, it's too cold to stay outside for very long, so this isn't a leisurely stroll, it's a business call, and as soon as Sophie finishes we high-tail it back across the street to Knitorious.

I unlock the front door and kick the snow off my boots against the brick wall next to it. Then I turn the knob and open the door, listening for the jingle of the bell, one of my favourite sounds.

Knitorious is warm and cozy and feels like home. Other than my house, it's the only place where walking through the door makes me feel both relaxed and reinvigorated at the same time.

I undo Sophie's leash and take her sweater off. She gives herself a shake, and follows me to the back room where I put our outerwear and her leash away. I freshen Sophie's water bowl, turn on the lights in the store, unlock the front door, and flip the sign from closed to open.

"It's showtime," I say to Sophie, just like Connie always says to me when she unlocks the door and turns the sign.

Tuesdays aren't our busiest day of the week, but we're in the midst of the winter tourist season, so I expect a steady flow of customers.

Despite Harmony Lake's small size, we squeeze in a large population of tourists during the winter and summer tourist seasons.

In the winter, tourists flock to the two ski resorts in the Harmony Hills Mountains, various rental houses, and the new condominium development at the end of Water Street, and in the summer, they flock to the same places for access to the lake and the small-town-living experience.

Besides being small, Harmony Hills is secluded which gives it the feeling of being further away from the hustle and bustle of the city than it is.

I can see the lake from the front window of the store, across the street, just beyond the park where I walked Sophie. Behind me, to the north, are the Harmony Hills Mountains. Tiny, as far as mountain ranges go, but a popular destination for weekend skiers and snowboarders. Geographically, Harmony Lake can't be a bigger town.

Not without moving either a lake or a small mountain range.

Knitorious is closed on Sundays and Mondays, so I spend Tuesdays returning phone calls and emails and processing online orders that were placed on the store website over the weekend. I turn on the laptop and, while waiting for it to power up, check the store voicemail.

The bell over the door jingles, and a well-wrapped Connie comes in from the cold.

"Good morning, Megan, my dear."

She always says it in a sing-song voice.

Sophie jumps up from her dog bed to greet Connie and is wagging her Corgi butt while she follows Connie to the back room.

"Good morning to you, too, Sophie," Connie sings from the back room.

Connie is my mother-friend, and I'm her daughter-friend.

We met sixteen years ago when Adam, Hannah, and I first moved to Harmony Lake. We became instant friends and soon after we became family.

I lost my mum just after Hannah's first birthday, and Hannah was born when I was barely twenty-one, so when Connie and I met, I was young, newly married, a new mum, and grieving. She welcomed us, nurtured us and filled the mother and grandmother-shaped holes we had in our hearts. At almost seventy years young, she's the most beautiful, smart, and sophisticated woman I know.

I started working here part-time about five years ago and became the store owner a few months ago when

Connie decided it was time for her to retire and move out of the upstairs apartment. She moved into a new condo with her boyfriend, Archie, and I took over as owner of Knitorious. So, now I own Knitorious and Connie works here part time. We've come full circle.

"Today feels bittersweet," Connie says as she crouches down to pet Sophie.

"I know. It'll be hard to let her go," I say, "It's been nice having a pet in the store again, and we fit together so well, you know? We're like kindred spirits. At home, we both like to eat, we both like to nap, and we both like to cuddle. At the store, we both like to greet the customers and visit with everyone. I'll miss her."

"Well, Archie and I are going south in a couple of weeks, so you'll have Harlow to help you run the store and keep you company while we're away. I know Laura has missed Sophie dearly and can't wait to see her."

Harlow is Connie's cat. When Connie owned the store and lived upstairs, Harlow had unrestricted access to both the store and the apartment. He was a fixture here. Even non-knitters would come in just to visit him. The store feels incomplete without him here, but I get custody of him when Connie and Archie travel, so he stays at Knitorious while they're away.

"Phillip said he's picking Laura up from the hospital and taking her home this morning. Once she's settled, I'll take Sophie home to her, "I explain. "According to Phillip, Laura's looking at six weeks in a cast, so he and I will work out a schedule where we take turns walking her — Sophie, I mean, not Laura."

Phillip Wilde is my neighbour. He owns Wilde Flowers, the florist next door to Knitorious, and he lives next door to me. We're work neighbours and home neighbours.

Ding! I have a text.

April: Coffee?

Me: Yes! Please!

April and I have been best friends since we met at a Mommy-and-Me group sixteen years ago. Her daughter, Rachel,and my Hannah are the same age and best friends. They're just starting their second semester of university in Toronto. April and her wife, Tamara, also have a son, Zach, who's fifteen, plays hockey, and eats them out of house and home, according to his mothers.

April and Tamara are the owners of Artsy Tartsy, the bakery up the street from Knitorious. Tamara is a talented pastry chef.

About ten minutes after we text, April arrives like a tall, blue-eyed, blonde angel bearing the gift of caffeine. She sets a tray of three to-go cups from the Latte Da café on the counter, then pulls off her mitts, puts them in her coat pockets, and pulls a paper bag from her coat pocket.

"Courtesy of T," she says, dropping the paper bag on the counter. "Dog treats from the latest test batch. We hope Sophie likes them."

I open the bag and remove a small, round, treat that looks like a tennis ball. Sophie is sitting at attention, staring intently at my hand with the treat in it.

She takes her role as taste tester seriously.

"Here you go, Soph!"

I toss the small treat onto her dog bed and she devours it.

"She likes it," I say to April.

Tamara is creating a line of organic, artisanal dog and cat treats to donate to the upcoming silent auction that will benefit our local animal shelter.

Connie and her friends are celebrating their fiftieth high school reunion soon and have decided to host a fundraising event that will be open to the entire town, and will benefit The Vanity Fur Centre for Animal Health & Wellness (us locals call it the Animal Centre or the AC, for short).

Most local businesses are donating items for the silent auction portion of the fundraiser, and April and Tamara are donating pet treats. At least they are if Tamara perfects a recipe she's happy with.

Sophie is part of their focus group and enjoys free samples in exchange for her opinion. Her opinion is always the same: more treats please!

"Have you decided what you're donating to the silent auction yet?" April asks me as she takes a coffee from the tray and hands it to Connie who's sitting on the sofa in the cozy sitting area of the store.

I nod while swallowing my first satisfying sip of coffee and feel its warmth spread through my body. "Yes. The winning bidder will get a bespoke pair of socks, hand knit by me, in a yarn of their choice."

Coffee in hand, I walk over to the cozy sitting area and join them on the comfy, overstuffed furniture.

"I've also been knitting baby blankets using leftover

yarn," I say, "for the charity knitting guild's donation to the AC. We have about ten so far. The AC uses them to line the kennels for the shelter animals, and for wrapping up preemie and sick animals to keep them warm."

"Who will be your date, my dear?" Connie asks.

Here we go.

"I'm a confident, independent woman who enjoys her own company and can attend a function alone," I reply.

To be honest, I haven't decided for sure if I'm going yet, but if I do I thought I might take Sophie as my plus one. I could knit her a little corgi-sized dress to wear. It is a fundraiser to benefit animals, after all. And her human, Laura is the founder and executive director of the AC, so it would be appropriate for Sophie to attend. But it might also be weird and earn me a crazy-dog lady label that I don't need.

"You should be dating!" Connie declares, throwing her hands into the air with dramatic flair.

Connie is a hand-talker and gesticulates as a way to visually punctuate when she speaks.

"Thirty-nine is too young to be alone. You should be having fun and meeting people," she says.

"And by people, I mean men," she clarifies, in case I don't know what she means.

April nods in agreement to everything Connie says. It's two against one.

"What do you think Detective Sergeant?" Connie asks, looking behind me. "Don't you agree that Megan is too young for a life of solitude?"

I turn around to see Eric standing near the counter.

He's blushing. I look back at Connie who has a look of smug enjoyment on her face for making him blush. She teases him about being shy when he is supposed to be a case-hardened cop.

Eric is my tenant. He lives in the apartment above the store and he's new to Harmony Lake.

Last fall, when Harmony Lake had it's first murder ever (technically, our first two murders), the Harmony Lake Police Department borrowed Eric Sloane from a larger department because they didn't have a major crimes unit.

After he solved both murders (with a little help) and prevented a third murder (mine), Harmony Lake implemented a major crimes unit and offered him a job. He is the major crimes unit. Just him.

He's forty-ish, divorced, no kids, and hot. Seriously, he's distractingly attractive. I've had to train myself to not stare.

"Hi Eric," I smile.

I walk over to the counter, silently thanking him for his good timing and interrupting an uncomfortable conversation.

"Hi Megan," He says. "Do you have a package for me?"

I tilt my head and raise my eyebrows. A package? Am I meant to have a package? Did I forget about a package for Eric? I shake my head.

"Phillip was supposed to drop off a package of hand-knit dog sweaters for me to pick up. Laura Pingle is donating them to the silent auction."

I shake my head, "No, Phillip hasn't dropped anything off."

"Amy is expecting me to bring it to the station today."

Officer Amy Andrews is organizing the silent auction portion of the fundraiser. The AC provides free veterinary care for PSD Tundra, Harmony Lake's police dog. Amy is his handler and supporting the AC is important to her. I've heard from some other business owners that she takes her role as organizer seriously. One person likened her to a bride on one of those Bridezilla reality shows.

"I'll text Phillip," I offer.

I text Phillip and ask if he has a package for Eric. While I'm waiting for a response, Connie asks April if there's been any more news about Mega Mart and the AC.

"When I was at the town council meeting in December, the council was divided right down the middle," April says, using her hand like a knife and slicing it through the air. "Laura was there, and she told the pro-Mega-Mart council members that a Mega Mart would go on that land 'over my dead body.' Those were her exact words. Then she said, 'not even over my dead body, because I intend to donate the land before I die to ensure it will always be The Vanity Fur Centre for Animal Health And Wellness.' Then she stomped out of the meeting."

April attends town council meetings on behalf of the Water Street Business Association (WSBA). Each year a different member takes a turn attending the meetings, reporting any relevant details to the rest of the WSBA, and advocating on our behalf.

Ding! I check my phone.

"Laura didn't give him anything for you," I tell Eric, "He says he dropped Laura off at home a couple of hours ago and is going back at lunch to check on her and take her some soup. He says he'll ask her about the sweaters then."

Eric rubs the back of his neck with his hand.

"I'm planning to walk over to Laura's house in a little while to drop off Sophie. I can ask her for the package and bring it back to the store, if that helps," I offer.

"Why don't I walk over there with you," he suggests, "It'll give me a chance to introduce myself and thank her personally. I'm still the new guy in town, and an introduction from an already-trusted community member like you is always helpful."

He crosses his arms in front of his chest. Don't stare at his chest, Megan.

"Also, I really don't want to show up at the station and see Amy without that package," he adds.

"You two should go now while I'm here to watch the store." Connie makes a sweeping motion with her hands to dismiss us.

"I guess I'll get Sophie and I bundled up," I say, shrugging.

"Great," Eric says, "I'll go get my coat.

PREORDER KILLER CABLES HERE: https://www.bklnk.com/B085WCF4K6

ABOUT THE AUTHOR

Reagan Davis doesn't really exist. She is a pen name for the real author who lives in the suburbs of Toronto with her husband, two kids, and a menagerie of pets. When she's not planning the perfect murder, she enjoys knitting, reading, eating too much chocolate, and drinking too much Diet Coke. The author is an established knitwear designer who regularly publishes individual patterns and is a contributor to many knitting books and magazines. I'd tell you her real name, but then I'd have to kill you. (Just kidding! Sort of.)

http://www.ReaganDavis.com/

ACKNOWLEDGMENTS

This book would not exist without the patience and grace of some very talented people.

Thank you to Kim's Covers for interpreting a vague, and ever-changing vision in my head, and turning it into the perfect cover.

Thank you to Chris and Sherry at The Editing Hall for removing all the double spaces, converting commas that should have been periods, and fixing my sentences when they run like they're being chased (see what I did there!).

Thank you to the beta readers for your honest feedback and patience.

Thank you to the Husbeast and Kidlets for your patience, without you this book would have been published six months sooner.

Made in the USA
Monee, IL
12 November 2020

47378641R00163